TO DECEIVE THEM

DI SAM COBBS
BOOK 16

M A COMLEY

To my mother, gone but never forgotten. Miss you every second of every day, Mum.

Also to my dear friend, Mary, I hope you found the peace you were searching for, lovely lady.

ACKNOWLEDGMENTS

Special thanks as always go to @studioenp for their superb cover design expertise.

My heartfelt thanks go to my wonderful editor Emmy, my proofreaders Joseph and Barbara for spotting all the lingering nits.

A special shoutout to all my wonderful ARC Group, who help to keep me sane.

PROLOGUE

Helen's excitement had finally given way to weariness. It had been a long day—no, week—and this morning's fire alarm going off before the function had started almost made it all crumble around her ears. But she had ventured on, fought the adversity threatening to spoil the day for everyone, and won, making this bridal fair a resounding success.

She circulated the great hall of the venue, which happened to be a castle she frequently visited at Muncaster, and breathed out a relieved sigh. She noted there was less tension in the room that had been fraught at times during the day. The exhibitors had worked well with her, mostly. There was the odd couple she had encountered over the years who never appeared to be happy, no matter how much she went out of her way to make things right for them.

"Hi, Helen," Crystal Lawler said, the lady who ran the only bridal boutique in the area. "Thanks for all your hard work in pulling this off today. I had my doubts about whether this place would draw in the crowds, but I should have trusted you. You were right, as usual."

"It's magical here, isn't it? So glad you're thrilled by the outcome, Crystal. Have you received many bookings?"

"About thirty, I think. We'll see how many turn up for their appointments, shall we?"

They both laughed, and then Helen continued her journey around the room. By this time, the stallholders had finished their celebratory glasses of fizz, which Helen had handed around, and were busy packing up their belongings.

Neil Kendrick, her boss, had arrived and was standing in the doorway, surveying the room. She swallowed the bile that had filled her mouth and set a smile in place as she drifted over to speak with him.

"Helen. It seems pretty quiet in here."

"Er... that's because all the customers have left. The event was scheduled to finish at four, and it's four-thirty now." She resisted the temptation to roll her eyes at his mistake.

"Ah, yes. I was just testing. How did it go?"

"I've spoken to most of the exhibitors, and they seem to think it went well. So I'm a happy bunny."

"Let's not count our chickens too quickly. I received a call stating that some of them weren't impressed with the way you handled the fire alarm incident earlier."

"Who told you that?"

He tapped the side of his nose. "I can't divulge that. I'm sorry. What happened?"

"It was out of my hands. A small fire started in the kitchen when they were preparing the nibbles. The manager dealt with everything swiftly, as expected. I checked that everyone was all right, and they all seemed happy enough to me. No one whinged about anything, not to my face, anyway."

"I wouldn't be here if someone hadn't raised a complaint."

She glanced over her shoulder to scour the room for anyone who was possibly observing them. They were all too busy packing away their merchandise to care. Which made Helen wonder if Neil was winding her up. She faced him again and shrugged. "I don't know what you expect me to do about the situation, if you're not willing to divulge who is intent on causing trouble for me."

Neil frowned and tilted his head. "Who said they were causing trouble for you?"

Her frustration twisted a knot in her stomach. "Are we done here?"

"Yes. Carry on."

She didn't need telling twice. *Thanks for souring my mood, Neil. Come again, won't you?*

Helen continued to circulate the room, checking if everyone was okay. All the exhibitors seemed friendly and happy enough for her. Neil could be a funny bugger at the best of times. But the fact that he had specifically travelled from their office in Workington to show up at the venue unnerved her. Something he'd never done before. Not that they'd received any complaints in the past.

She continued to do the rounds, ensuring everyone was happy until the last person left the great hall. The manager, Gemma Smith, came to find her as she was waving off the final exhibitor.

"I can't apologise enough for the fire happening this morning, Helen. I hope it didn't cause too much of a distraction for you."

"No, I didn't think it had. But someone must have rung the office and put in a complaint, that's why my boss showed up."

"Oh, goodness. It doesn't take much for someone to try to ruin the day for others, does it? Send them my way. I'll arrange for a free family day out for them. It was our fault, not yours."

"I can handle it, but thank you for the offer. It means a lot. This place is stunning. I'm delighted we decided to hold the event here, and you and your staff have been exceptional, catering for our every need. I'll bear you in mind for future events."

They shook hands, and Helen went back to the small room they had provided for her, where she could keep her coat and handbag. She collected them and then drove home.

Neil was nowhere to be seen, and his car wasn't among the others when she got back to her vehicle. *What a strange man he is. He shows up here, gives me a rollicking, and then buggers off without even announcing his departure.*

During her journey, she was forced to shield her eyes from the sun dipping in the west at the end of its long day. Spring had sprung, at last, putting the dreary months of winter behind them.

Helen parked and walked across the cobbled driveway, the chill of the Lake District's evening air reminding her that it was still early March as it nipped at her skin. She fumbled with her keys, cursing when her bag slipped off her shoulder. Inside, the house was quiet, too quiet. Her husband, Jason, was away on business for the week, attending an accountancy refresher course, as he had called it, in Carlisle. He'd left first thing yesterday. Planted a kiss on her cheek and displayed a forced smile that had, for some reason, made her shudder. Always playing the perfect husband. But the chinks were starting to show after ten years of marriage. His smile no longer fooled her.

She removed her coat and shoes in the hallway and glanced around the dimly lit house, the last rays of sunshine shining through the upstairs window on the landing, flooding the hallway. However, she felt there was something wrong. Something gnawing at her insides. She rubbed at her neck, ridding herself of the sensation that an invisible noose had been attached.

Helen had never been subjected to so much anxiousness in her home before. *What the heck is going on? Is this all because Neil showed up at the location?* She jumped as her phone vibrated in her jacket pocket. She removed it, the screen lit up, and she read the text message.

WARREN: *Missed you today. Still thinking about last night...*

"DAMN. LEAVE ME ALONE." Her heart skipped several beats, and a pang of guilt swiftly consumed her. She stared at the words, her fingers trembling, hovering over the buttons. She wondered whether she should reply or leave it a while until she got her head straight. Her confusion intensified when she recounted what had happened over the past few days. If she had the chance to rewind time, she'd do it in a heartbeat.

The arguments she'd had with Jason over the last couple of weeks had taken their toll on her, sending her into the arms of another man. Now, she was riddled with guilt. Their once strong marriage was now in tatters, at least in her eyes. *Why did I do it? Why did I meet up with Warren, knowing where it would lead? He's the polar opposite of Jason, young and exciting, whereas Jason has become staid in life.* Or so she believed. She paused to consider the dilemma, not for the first time that day.

While the event had been a success and kept her mind off Warren, there were lingering doubts tearing through her mind. Receiving his text only seemed to heighten her feelings again.

Warren was different, and it was that difference that had tempted her into the hotel bedroom with him the previous evening. She sighed, her mind whirling up a storm of confusion. Without replying —she couldn't hold the conversation with him, not tonight—she walked through to the kitchen, poured herself a glass of Cabernet Sauvignon and sat on the window seat overlooking her impressive garden at the rear. She loved this place. Walking through the front door usually wrapped her in a safety blanket, so why had that feeling evaded her this evening? She hated the capabilities of her thoughts at times. Why couldn't she live a normal life like her friends? Why did her life always need to feel complicated? Her mind raced. A new quandary had surfaced the second Warren had seduced her. Now she had two men in her life, which added to her confusion.

A cold shiver tickled her spine, and the silence grew louder around her. After a moment's hesitation, she withdrew her phone again. This time, she dialled Jason's number. It rang twice before he answered.

"Hi, what's up?" he said, his voice muffled, giving the impression that he was preoccupied.

"Hey," Helen said casually. "I just wanted to check in with you. How is the course going?"

A long pause filled the line. "It's going well, or should I say, it's okay. There's a lot to take in." His tone was cold, almost distant.

Unless that was her imagination playing tricks on her. "You sound distracted." She glanced at the clock on the wall and was shocked to learn it was almost seven already. "Are you sure everything is okay?"

"Yes, I'm sure. I'm pooped, tired beyond words. I'm not used to being back in a classroom; it has come as a culture shock to me. I'll call you tomorrow. I'll be more used to it by then," he replied quickly.

Helen picked up on his eagerness to end their conversation. She bit her lip. She knew him well enough to know when something wasn't right. But what more could she say?

"Okay, if you're sure?" she murmured, the disconnect pronounced between them. "Goodnight, Jason. Sleep well."

"Goodnight."

The line went dead, putting an abrupt end to their conversation. No going back and forth between them, saying endless goodbyes like they used to do at the start of their relationship. She sipped at her wine and wondered when everything had started to go wrong. Helen struggled to pinpoint the exact time, which galled her. She loved Jason; at least, she thought she did. She often pondered how deep that love went. What lengths either of them would be prepared to go to if they were asked to prove it. She wasn't sure and doubted whether he would be either, what with their relationship being in tatters. Guilt, the dominant emotion, whipped up a frenzy in her mind.

The night had descended faster than she'd expected. The solar lights had kicked in on the patio area, but it wasn't enough for her to see properly. She left her seat and topped up her glass, then opened the fridge to contemplate what to have for dinner.

She had betrayed Jason and now she was left wondering if she would be able to live with the guilt. Taking her glass with her, she wandered through to the lounge and lit the fire in the grate. Then she tore upstairs to get out of her work clothes. She paused at the top and glanced back down the stairs. *Will the fire be safe if I have a bath?*

After deliberating the question for the next few seconds, she took a punt that it would be and walked into the bathroom to run the bath.

Then she collected her velour pyjamas from the bedroom and, drink in hand, sat on the toilet seat, watching the water filling the tub, bringing with it a cloud of bubbles.

Mesmerised by what was going on in front of her, Helen let her mind drift back to her predicament. Should she give Warren the go-ahead and answer his text, or would it be wiser to let him go and concentrate on getting her marriage back on track?

The bubbles spilt over the lip of the bath. Her phone buzzed again, adding to the pressure on her shoulders. Warren was being impatient with her, which in itself raised an alarm.

Warren: Can't wait to see you again...

HELEN'S LIPS curved into a bittersweet smile as she set the phone on the floor beside her. Maybe, just maybe, Warren was the escape she needed—the distraction she was after with Jason being so distant.

She soaked for longer than she'd anticipated and then slipped into her pyjamas and went back downstairs. She was feeling peckish but unsure of what she wanted to eat. After throwing a log on the dying embers in the grate, she went through to the kitchen to recheck the contents of her fridge. She'd picked at the buffet food all day and was aware of the calories she'd consumed. Finally, she decided to knock herself up a cheese and tomato omelette, which she ate sitting at the island in the kitchen. Afterwards, her thoughts returned to her problem. She reached for her mobile, which was sitting beside her, and toyed with the idea of whether to call Warren or not, but something prevented her.

A noise sounded in the pantry. She jumped off her stool to investigate. She pushed the door open and leapt back, the smell of petrol hitting her as smoke entered the kitchen. "What the fuck?" She ran back to retrieve her phone and called nine-nine-nine. "Help, please, you have to help me. My house is on fire, and I don't know what to do."

"Okay, ma'am. Please, try to remain calm. Where are you?"

"Twenty-two Grassmere Road in Harrington. Please, tell me what to do."

"Can you isolate the fire?"

"I opened the door to the pantry, and the flames were lashing up the front of the cupboards." The smoke hit her lungs, making her cough.

"Can you close the door again to try to contain the fire in one place?"

"I can try." She reached for the handle, which was made of metal, and screamed as the heat singed her palm.

"Are you okay?" the operator asked. "Don't worry, the fire brigade is on their way. Just get out of the house."

"I can't. It's all I have. If I lose my home, I'll have nothing."

"You can't think that way. You need to leave the residence right away. Go to a neighbour's house if you can."

"I can't. I don't want to leave my home." Then her phone ran out of battery; hardly surprising, considering the number of panicked calls she'd made during the day. *Shit, I should have charged it in the car on the way home.* She ran the cold-water tap, filled the washing-up bowl with it, and then threw it on the fire. The flames died down, only to bounce back. Panic took over. She ran through the house, collecting her laptop and handbag—the two things that meant the most to her in the world—and opened the front door to leave, only to find a figure dressed in black standing on the other side.

She screamed and retreated into the hallway. The person raised the hammer they were holding and bludgeoned her with it. She sank to the marble-tiled floor, and her life flashed before her eyes.

They flickered shut, never to open again.

1

"What a mess," DI Sam Cobbs muttered when she got out of the car.

Her partner, DS Bob Jones, let out a long, low whistle and a few choice expletives.

They moved closer to the charred remains of the detached house and stopped to show their ID and sign the log sheet upon their arrival at the cordon.

The young male officer handed Sam the clipboard and said, "Morning, ma'am. The fire brigade has just finished putting out the last of the flames. They've told me to advise anyone arriving on site to take extra precautions when entering."

"They're still here, though, right?"

"Yes, the last engine is around the back."

"Is that where the fire started?" Sam asked. She took a gamble that the flames had surfaced in the kitchen, which was most likely to be located at the rear of the property.

"Yes, it appears so, ma'am."

"Thanks, we'll head round there and have a chat with whoever is in charge. Have SOCO been called? Do you know if there was anyone inside when the fire started?"

"I'm not sure if they've discovered anyone or not. I've been ensuring the neighbours remain behind the tape."

"Okay, continue the good work."

Sam ducked under the crime scene tape, followed by Bob who was already grumbling under his breath.

"What's wrong with you?"

"The stench is getting to me already. I can just imagine what it's doing to the fibres of my new suit."

"Goodness me. Are you for real? Stop whining, man. What if someone has lost their life in the fire? And here you are, complaining…"

"All right. There's no need for you to go overboard. You shouldn't have asked me what was wrong if you couldn't handle the answer."

Sam shook her head and walked down the side of the building.

Four firemen were packing up their equipment, getting ready to leave.

Sam flashed her ID. "Hi, I'm DI Sam Cobbs, the SIO on the investigation. Can you give me any information about how the fire probably started?"

"We're going to need to leave the actual assessment to the fire assessor, however, what I can tell you is that an accelerant was used."

"Accelerant? Any idea what that might have been?"

"The obvious would be petrol. We could smell it when we entered the kitchen area."

"Okay, thanks. Any bodies found inside?"

"Yes, a woman by the front door."

"Oh. Do you think she was trying to leave the property? Escape the fire?"

"I'd say that was a given," replied the fireman, who was in his fifties.

"Was she overwhelmed by the smoke?" Sam asked. Something told her that wasn't the case, given the fireman's expression.

He tutted, inhaled a breath and said, "Sadly, no. She had several head injuries and no sign of anything falling on her. Also, the door was open when we got here."

Shocked, Sam shook her head. "Okay, I believe SOCO and the pathologist are on their way. Are you going now?"

"Yes, we've got another call to attend as backup. I rang the assessor. He's about ten minutes away. He told us to get on the road."

"I agree. We'll hang around for a while, anyway. Thanks for all you've done here today."

"It's never good to lose someone."

"I know."

Sam and Bob took a few steps towards the back of the house. The odour was more intense on this side of the building.

"Do you know the property?" Sam asked.

"I've passed it a few times. It used to be a white cottage with a thatched roof, which would explain why the roof and most of the walls are gone. Such a shame."

"I've never seen such devastation. I hate house fires, especially when an accelerant has been used." Sam tightened her coat around her, warding off the bite of the wind that had suddenly picked up. But it wasn't just the cold that made her shiver. Fires like this didn't just happen and, Sam quickly realised this was a murder investigation with the homeowner possibly found with wounds to the head.

Beside her, Bob shifted uncomfortably, his expression grim as he stared at the destruction. His jaw tightened, and Sam knew he was thinking the same thing as her.

"Someone was determined to make the fire spread out of control quickly. Was that to cover up the murder? Was the woman killed before the fire was started?"

"I suppose that's up to Des and his team to find out for us."

The sound of rustling rounded the corner behind them. "Good morning," Des Markham said brightly. "Wow, this is going to take some sifting through."

Three team members, all carrying bags of equipment, came to a halt behind them.

"Where do we stand?" Des asked.

"The fire assessor should be here any second. I had a word with the team before they left. A woman's body was found inside the building near the front door, indicating head injuries but no signs of debris impact."

Des shrugged. "I'll be the judge of that. I find that hard to believe, given the state of the building."

"The thought also crossed my mind, but the fireman I spoke to was adamant."

"You can leave us to it. I presume we're free to enter the building."

Sam shrugged. "I'd be inclined to wait until the assessor arrived, but it's your call." She smiled and nudged her partner. "We'll wait around the front for him or her to arrive."

She and Bob returned to the front of the house. He was surprisingly quiet. She could tell he was distracted, his thoughts somewhere else entirely. He had been acting off since they'd arrived at the scene, his usually sharp focus possibly dulled by something personal. Sam followed his gaze to the crowd that had gathered just beyond the police tape, their murmurs barely audible over the sound of the wind. Neighbours, concerned locals and a few reporters had arrived, all watching the wreckage with morbid curiosity.

Just beyond them, a car came screeching around the corner, and the tyres smoked as it stopped in front of the tape. A man, his hair dishevelled, leapt out of the car.

"No!" he shouted.

"Shit!" Bob mumbled beside her.

"What's going on, Bob? Tell me. Now."

"I thought I recognised the address when we pulled up, but I couldn't be a hundred percent sure. That's Jason Flintoff, one of my best friends."

"What? Why didn't you tell me?"

He sighed and shrugged. "I didn't want to consider it being true. They moved here a few months ago, so I wasn't sure of the address. Sorry, I didn't keep it from you intentionally."

Sam ran a hand around her face. "You're going to have to deal with him."

"I can't do that. Don't ask me to do that, Sam. I'm begging you."

"Christ," she said under her breath. "I can't believe this is happening."

"Yeah, you're not the only one."

"Come on, we'd better have a word before he causes a scene."

"What? Isn't he entitled to do that after losing his wife?" Bob countered, his feet planted in the same spot.

"Pack it in, Bob. You're not thinking rationally here. First of all, the victim hasn't been identified as his wife. I have no intention of informing him she is dead, not until Des has confirmed it's her."

"And secondly?"

She glared at him. "There isn't one, not really, other than that we need to remain professional at all times. Whether the victims are known to us or not. You know that, I shouldn't have to remind you."

"I know." He sucked in a breath and then let it out. "I'm ready."

"Hey, Bob, over here," the man shouted.

The officer at the cordon was having difficulty restraining him.

Sam upped her pace and said, "It's all right, Officer. We've got this."

"What's going on here, and where is my wife?" the man asked.

"All right, Jason, calm down, mate. We've not long arrived ourselves," Bob told him.

"Bob, would you mind introducing us?"

"Jason Flintoff, this is my partner, DI Sam Cobbs. She'll be the Senior Investigating Officer."

"So... what can you tell me? Apart from the fact that my house no longer exists?"

"As Bob has already told you, we've only just arrived, and so has SOCO, which means that any information we're likely to gather won't be available for a long time. Is there somewhere you can go to stay with a friend or relative? We'll contact you later."

"No. I mean, yes. But I don't want to leave here, not until I know if my wife is alive or not." He glanced sideways at the drive. "Her car is here, so I assume she was inside."

"When was the last time you spoke to her?"

"Last night from my hotel."

Sam tilted her head. "Your hotel? Had you had an argument?"

"No. I was away on a course. I left two days ago. We spoke on the phone last night."

"Ah, okay. Can you tell us which hotel you were staying at?"

Bob removed his notebook from his pocket slower than normal, as if reluctant to jot down the information.

"The Crest Hotel in Carlisle."

"Thank you. May I ask how you learnt about the fire?"

"One of my mates rang me." He pointed at the house across the street. "Phil. He tried to help but was beaten back by the flames. The fire brigade showed up and took over. I'm grateful to him for attempting to save Helen's life."

"Did Phil tell you that Helen was definitely inside the property?" Sam asked.

"Yes, he saw her arrive home earlier in the evening. Please, why can't you tell me if you've found her or not?"

"All we can do is pass on what we were told when we arrived."

Jason frowned and demanded, "Which was?"

"A female was found in the hallway, close to the front door."

"Close to the front door? Why didn't she make it out of the building? Don't tell me she decided to grab that damn laptop of hers and got caught!"

"That's as much as we know at present. It would be wrong of me to speculate, not having assessed the scene for myself."

"When will I know?"

"Once SOCO and the pathologist have examined the inside of the property. At the moment, we're waiting for the fire assessor to arrive."

He glanced at what remained of his home and shook his head. "People warned us of the dangers, the risks of having a thatched roof. I guess that's come back and bitten me in the arse, hasn't it? How did the fire start?"

"We don't know, mate," Bob said, finally finding his voice.

"Why not? It's your frigging job to know, Bob," Jason snapped. He stamped his foot and turned away from them. Then he flung an apology over his shoulder.

"You're going to have to be patient, Jason. I know that's not what you want to hear at this time, but it's the best we can do for now. Why don't you leave us to it and go stay with a friend or family member? I promise I'll call you as soon as we know anything. I promise."

When Jason faced them again, tears were bulging, and he swiped them away with his hands. "Sorry for being such a dick. I'll sit in my car, ring a few mates. I don't think I could stand going to a family member's house and getting the third degree."

"We can appreciate that," Sam said. "As Bob said, the minute we hear anything, you'll be the first to know."

"Thanks," he muttered, and with a final look at the house, he walked away from them.

"Shit! I feel so bad for him," Bob whispered.

"I can understand that, Bob, but you're going to have to set your personal feelings aside; otherwise, you know as well as I do that they're likely to cloud any judgements you might make further down the line."

"That's bullshit and you know it, Sam. I would never let that happen."

Sam raised an eyebrow. "How many times have you been in this situation before?"

"I haven't."

"Then how can you confidently tell me that it won't happen?"

"Bugger. Okay, you've got me there. Anyway, my word should be enough."

Another car drew up, and a man got out and went to the boot of his vehicle. He slipped on a protective suit and then approached the cordon to sign in. "I'm Terry Lord, the fire assessor. Are you the officer in charge?" he asked Bob.

Bob jerked his thumb in Sam's direction. "No, my partner is."

Sam smiled at Lord. "DI Sam Cobbs of the Cumbria Constabulary. I'm the SIO on the investigation."

"I need access to the building before your lot go in there."

"Okay, we've got SOCO and the pathologist around the back.

They're waiting for you to give them the go-ahead to enter the building."

"I'll have a word with them. I won't permit them, not for at least an hour."

"Yikes. You're going to need to inform the pathologist as soon as you see him. I'm telling you now, he won't be happy."

"Tough. It's procedure. First, I need to ensure the building is safe."

He ducked under the tape and walked around the side of the building.

"Good luck telling Des that, pal," Bob said. "What now?"

"We should speak to the neighbours if they're willing to talk to us. In particular, I'm keen to hear what Phil has to say."

"Ah, but which house does he live in?" Bob queried.

"We'll ask around. We'll split up. I'll take this side. You take the residents over that side of the street."

"Are you kidding? There are dozens of onlookers to sift through. Can't we get backup out here?"

"Don't panic, I was about to suggest the same." She turned her back on the crowd and spoke to the desk sergeant at the station. "Nick, it's DI Cobbs at the scene of the fire. Can you arrange for a patrol to come out and give us a hand?"

"Consider it done, ma'am. Is it really bad out there?"

"As bad as it can get. I don't want to go into detail over the phone. I have wagging ears listening."

"I understand. Leave it with me. A team will be with you within ten minutes."

"You're amazing. Thanks, Nick." She hung up and caught something being said over to her right.

"Well, I'm not surprised, to be honest," a woman's voice whispered sharply near the cordon. "That marriage was falling apart. It was only a matter of time."

Sam's head snapped in the direction of the voice. Two women stood close to the edge of the tape, arms crossed, talking in hushed tones. One of them, a middle-aged woman with a concerned frown, was clearly more agitated than the other.

"You don't say things like that, Margaret!" her friend muttered back, glancing nervously at the house. "Not now, not after something as devastating as this has happened."

Sam discreetly inched closer to the women, her head bowed, pretending to write in her notebook.

"Why not?" Margaret said, her voice rising slightly. "We all heard them, didn't we? Arguing late at night. That poor girl… She must've been at her wits' end with him."

Sam's gut tightened. She took another few steps closer, trying not to make it obvious that she was listening in.

"He wasn't exactly subtle about it either," Margaret continued. "Not that I'm saying anything, but you don't need to be a genius to work out that there were problems. It wasn't the first time we heard raised voices coming from that house."

The friend shushed Margaret, but Sam had heard enough. A knot of suspicion coiled tighter in her chest.

Sam smiled and approached the women. "Hello, ladies. I assume you live close by. Is that correct?"

"Yes, Margaret and I live next door to each other. This is my house, the one two doors down from the Flintoffs'. I'm glad their house was detached. A fire hazard, those damn thatches, an accident waiting to happen if you ask me."

"Hush now, Daisy, the officer doesn't want to hear your opinion on owning a thatched cottage. It was pretty enough, in its own way. Or it used to be, when Mr and Mrs Potts had it."

Sam frowned. "Meaning?"

"Margaret, don't be so ridiculous," Daisy said.

"I'd like to hear what you have to say, Margaret."

The woman looked Sam up and down and said, "And you are?"

Sam produced her warrant card for the woman to read. "DI Sam Cobbs, the SIO on the investigation." She removed her notebook from her pocket.

"Oh, a woman in charge, eh? I bet that doesn't happen that often."

Sam smiled. "You'd be surprised. I overheard you talking. Were you saying that the Flintoffs often argued?"

The women glanced at each other and nodded.

"More often than not, especially over the last month or so. That's right, isn't it, Daisy?"

"Yes. We try to block our ears to it, but that's hard to do when they chase each other out to their cars, still screaming at each other," Daisy said.

"Oh dear, that doesn't sound good at all. Can you tell me what the arguments were about?" Sam asked.

"No, not really. We reckon either one of them was cheating on the other. That's usually the case, isn't it?"

"Possibly. About the fire... did you see anything suspicious last night?"

"Around what time?" Margaret asked.

"Ah, I can't give you a definitive time."

"Well, I put the bins out at about eight last night," Margaret said, her eyes screwed up as she thought. "Actually, I did see someone lingering on the corner." She pointed across the road, at the junction to the next street. "I didn't think anything of it at the time, assumed the person was waiting for a lift or something like that."

"Was it a man or a woman?"

"I don't know. They had one of those sweatshirts with the hood on, not sure what they're called."

"A hoodie," Sam suggested.

"Yes, that's the one."

"Thanks, that's helpful. Anything else out of the ordinary that you can think of from the last few months?"

"Nothing, except for the arguments. How much do you know about them?" Margaret asked.

"Very little at this stage. Mr Flintoff informed us that he was away on a course; he also said he left two days ago. Can you confirm that?"

The ladies looked at each other again.

"Maybe," Daisy agreed. "Hard to say, really."

"I think so," Margaret confirmed.

"Can I ask you ladies to give us a statement? We have a team on their way out here. They'll be dealing with that side of things."

"Can we do it together?" Daisy asked. She seemed fearful at the request.

"No, they need to be taken separately. Honestly, there's nothing to be scared of. All we'll need from you is what you've just told me and any other information you can think of in the meantime."

Daisy sighed. "Okay, if that's all it is."

Sam said farewell to the ladies and continued along the line of onlookers. A reporter popped up behind an elderly man who Sam was interested in speaking to.

"DI Cobbs, nice to see you again. What can you tell us about the fire?" the journalist asked.

Although Sam recognised him, she couldn't remember his name. All she knew was that he was from the local paper. She pointed to the end of the line. "I'll talk with you over there."

The journalist grinned and shoved the elderly gentleman in the back in his eagerness to move.

"Bloody cheek! Who the hell does he think he is?" the man complained.

"Sorry, sir," Sam said. "That was unacceptable. I'll have a word with him."

"Tell him from me that if I were thirty years younger, I would have thumped him."

Sam suppressed the giggle and nodded. "I'll let him know."

She moved along the line, not in any rush to get to the enthusiastic reporter. "Now, that was uncalled for, treating that elderly gentleman like that. When I've finished talking to you, I want you to go back there and apologise to him. Is that clear?"

"Yes." He rolled his eyes. "If I have to."

Sam shrugged. "Either you give me your word, or I'll refuse to hold a conversation with you. What's it to be?"

"Okay, okay, whatever, it makes no odds to me."

Sam resisted the temptation to smack him around the face. "Let's move on, shall we?"

"I think that's sensible. What can you tell us about the fire?"

By this time, several other journalists had joined them.

Sam cleared her throat. "This is a brief statement. I won't be making another one until I have spoken with the pathologist." She inwardly cringed at her mistake. She should have said SOCO.

The cheeky journalist was the first to react. "Pathologist? You're telling us there's a body inside the house?"

"I didn't say that. The pathologist has been called in as a precaution."

"Ah, right. Covering your back there nicely, I see. What about the homeowner? That's him over there, isn't it?" The same journalist nodded in the direction of the distraught Jason sitting in his vehicle.

"Leave him alone. He's in shock… as you can imagine, finding his house burnt down."

"Where was he when 'the accident' happened?"

"That's his business. I'm afraid that's all I have for you at this time. I need to see what the fire assessor has to say about the incident. I'd also like to add, or plead with you, to keep this off the air for now, just until things become clearer."

"No can do, sorry. The editor is eager for us to run the story. I'll name you in the article if that'll help."

The red mist descended. "You really think having my name in print matters to me? I'm a police officer. My job is to right the wrongs in our society, not to jump on the bandwagon and seek notoriety from the local press. Am I making myself clear?"

"Yes, Inspector," a few of the other journalists replied, but the cheeky one kept his mouth shut.

Sam noticed the twinkle in his eye. She heaved out a sigh and turned on her heel.

To get away from a further onslaught from the journalists, she crossed the road to check how Bob was getting on.

"How's it going?"

"I've had better days."

"Take a break. See how Jason is holding up."

Bob peered over his shoulder. "Do I have to?"

"Help me out here, partner. My back is against the wall, and you're crumbling before my eyes."

He puffed out his cheeks and shook his head. "That's a slight exaggeration."

"It's up to you. One thing I think you should know."

"What's that?"

"I've spoken to two of Jason's immediate neighbours, and they informed me that he and his wife, Helen, often argued."

"Did they? How certain are you that it's not hearsay from a couple of nosey neighbours?"

"I'm not certain, far from it. That's why I need you to have a word with him. If you don't, I'll have no alternative but to ask him to attend an interview at the station."

"Jesus, he doesn't even know if his wife is dead yet."

"Neither do we," Sam admitted. She walked off and made her way around the back of the building again to see what was going on with the forensic team and if they'd yet been allowed access to the building. What she hadn't realised was that Jason had left his vehicle and followed her.

She heard Jason's voice break as he muttered something.

"It's my fault," he whispered. "I wasn't here…"

Bob appeared and stood beside Sam. "Jason, you couldn't have known," he cut in, raw emotion in his voice. "This wasn't your fault."

Sam remained silent, watching the reactions of both men. There was something about the way Jason was acting. He was distant but not quite distraught. She had seen grief manifest in many ways, but this felt… different.

"Mr. Flintoff," Sam interrupted gently, stepping closer. "I understand this is an incredibly difficult time, but we need to ask you a few questions about Helen and what's happened here."

Jason's gaze flicked to Sam, his eyes bloodshot but dry. "What do you mean? It was a fire, wasn't it?"

Sam held his gaze, unflinching. "We're still investigating the cause, but it spread unusually fast. Do you know if anything in the house could have contributed to that?"

Jason frowned and shook his head. "No. No, everything was fine. We had an open fire; we burnt logs in the grate. Sometimes Helen refused to light it when she was alone..." His voice trailed off and his eyes clouded with something unreadable.

Sam noticed the shift immediately, and with her instincts on high alert, she pushed ahead, seeking answers. "Did something happen between you two recently? An argument, maybe?"

Jason's jaw tightened, and for the first time, there was a flicker of anger in his eyes. "What are you trying to say?"

"We're waiting on the pathologist's and SOCO's reports. At this moment, we don't know what caused the fire."

Bob stepped in quickly, raising a hand. "Calm down, mate. No one is suggesting anything. We just need to understand what went on in the lead-up to the fire."

But Sam wasn't about to let the question drop so easily. There was more to this—there had to be. She could feel it.

"I think that's enough for now," Bob said, and he shot Sam a warning glance. "Let's give him some time to come to terms with... what's happened, yeah?"

Sam hesitated but nodded, though her mind was already racing ahead. Something wasn't adding up. Her suspicions were growing by the second. What was behind the recent arguments? There was definitely something deeper going on behind closed doors.

Then Jason surprised Sam by asking, "Can I go in there?"

Sam raised an eyebrow at her partner as if expecting him to give the obvious answer.

"Not yet, Jason. Let the experts do their work for now. Come on, I'll see you back to your car."

Reluctantly, Jason allowed Bob to steer him back towards the front of the property. Sam's mind raced. *Why was he so eager to get inside? Ordinarily, I would accept it, but not after a fire of this size. I wouldn't want to go near my home if the devastation was this bad.* Even she was hesitant about entering the building.

She approached the back door and called out, "Des, is it safe for us to come in yet?"

There was no reply, but then the fire assessor appeared in the doorway. "I need to get something out of the car. Yes, you can enter the building, just don't disturb anything. However, I would still suggest wearing a protective suit."

Sam wouldn't have thought it necessary, given the state of the building. Rather than argue, she walked with him back to their vehicles.

Bob joined her. "What are you up to?" he asked, his tone clipped.

She selected two plastic bags containing suits and threw one at him. "That much should be obvious. And cut the crap; don't forget who you're talking to."

He mumbled an apology and stared at the suit. "We're going in? Why?"

"Why? Do you really need to ask that?"

"Please don't snap my head off; it was a simple question."

Sam stepped into her suit and at the same time tried to calm herself. "I need to see what's going on inside the house. My advice to you would be to forget Jason is your friend and get on with your job."

"Really? I have been taking it seriously. What are you saying?"

"That you're not thinking objectively at the moment. That needs to change, Bob, or you and I are going to fall out. If you're telling me you're not up to the task, I can ring the station and get another team member to switch places with you."

"What? There's no need for that, not unless you're telling me to back off."

"I'm not." She sighed and stared back at the building. "We need to treat this case seriously. Someone has lost their life in there. The likelihood is that the person is Jason's wife; that's all the more reason for us to do our best to find out how the fire started and whether it was set on purpose."

"The fireman told us he smelt petrol. What more do you need to know?"

"You're not thinking straight. Maybe Helen took a canister of petrol into the property with her, but it doesn't mean someone set fire to the cottage on purpose. That's why we need to let SOCO and the fire assessor do their thing, of course. I'm all for keeping an open mind for now until someone can prove how the fire began. I think you should do the same."

Bob shrugged into his suit and nodded. "You're the one under the impression that I'm not open-minded."

Sam pressed her key fob to lock the doors, and together they returned to the back of the house in silence. En route, she glanced in Jason's direction. He was sitting in his car, watching their every move, which unnerved her.

The fire assessor followed them. He entered the building first. "I shouldn't need to tell you to tread carefully. Try not to disturb anything as you proceed through the building."

Sam and Bob glanced at each other and rolled their eyes.

She replied, "Of course. We'll do our best."

They wound their way through the kitchen and into the hallway, where Des was crouching over the body. Hearing them approach, he looked up.

"What can you tell us, Des?"

The team had erected a couple of lights to brighten the area. Even though the front door was open, the flames had charred the hallway.

"The wounds were inflicted prior to her death. My suggestion would be that she opened the door to someone, and they instantly attacked her, possibly with a hammer. Although, saying that, there's no sign of the weapon in the area; the techs have checked."

"Ouch. Then the murderer tried to cover their tracks by setting the fire. Is that it?"

"More than likely. The assessor believes an accelerant was used. You can smell it as you enter the building at the rear."

"Yes, we noticed that." Sam peered over her shoulder. "So, the murderer wanted us to believe the fire started in the kitchen, like eight out of ten house fires in this country, I suspect." She crossed the hallway and studied the doorframe outside. "No doorbell camera, from what I can tell."

"Yes, that's right. That was the first thing I checked for myself," Des agreed.

"We've spoken to some of the neighbours. One of them told me she saw a figure standing on the corner of the road when she was putting the bins out last night. She didn't think anything of it at the time, thought they were waiting for a lift. The person was wearing a hoodie, so she couldn't tell if they were male or female."

"Did the neighbours see what time she got home? Or when the fire started?"

"No, it's all a bit sketchy. I think most of them are in shock. I've got a team coming out to take down their statements. We'll sift through them and see if anything comes to light there. I take it it's going to be impossible to give us a time of death?"

"At this time, yes. I'd like to get her moved ASAP and back to the lab to carry out the PM. I don't see the point of staying here to make the assessment."

"I'm inclined to agree with you. I want you to be aware that the husband is sitting out front in his car."

"Is he likely to make a fuss?" Des got to his feet and asked.

"We can hang around, ensure that doesn't happen, if you want. Jason is Bob's friend."

"Oh, you have my condolences, Bob. Did you know his wife?"

Bob's gaze shifted to the victim. "Not that well. I met her at the wedding. You know how it is."

Sam frowned. "Really? I got the impression that your friendship was pretty solid," she said.

"It is."

Sam and Des shared a look that said otherwise.

She decided not to press the matter further. "Additionally, some of the immediate neighbours heard the couple arguing recently."

"That doesn't mean anything," Bob responded swiftly. "Couples raise their voices at each other all the time."

"But most of the time, it doesn't end in murder," Sam retorted quickly, without engaging her brain. "Sorry, I didn't mean to sound so insensitive."

Bob turned and walked back into the kitchen.

"Bugger, I think I've put my foot in it again. All right if I check he's okay?"

"Feel free. We'll get the body bagged up if I can ask you to keep the husband occupied for the next ten minutes or so."

"Consider it done. Let me know the results of the post-mortem ASAP, if you would?"

"Don't I always?"

"You're a good man, Des."

He grinned. "I know."

Sam picked her way through the debris and back through the kitchen to find her partner. He was outside, leaning against the wall, his hands resting on his knees.

She patted him on the shoulder. "I'm sorry. I'm sensing anything I say right now is being taken the wrong way."

"No, it should be me apologising. It's about Jason," Bob began. "I get that you're suspicious, but we have to be careful all the same. He's just lost his wife, for God's sake. I know he's my mate, but let's set that aside for a moment. He's come home to find his house destroyed, and for all he knows, his wife dead, not that we've confirmed that to him yet. I know him; he's not capable of doing something like this."

Sam leaned against the wall beside him. "You're going to have to detach yourself from the fact that he's your friend, Bob. Start assessing the situation as if he were a stranger. Don't you think it's suspicious that he hasn't left yet? We gave him explicit instructions to stay with friends or family, to leave the scene."

Bob straightened and pushed himself away from the wall. "Come on, Sam; you'd react exactly the same way. I know you would. Give the guy a break."

"I can't. His wife has been murdered. You know as well as I do, the husband is always the first person we suspect in instances like this. The fact that he was away on a course when the fire happened should also be a red flag for us. Normally, it would be. That's why I think you should take a step back, let me partner up with another member of the team."

"I can't. I owe it to Jason to be involved in the case—to find out how Helen died, or should I say, was murdered."

"I get the need for you to do that... all right, I'll allow you to continue to work the case alongside me on one proviso."

"Which is?"

"That you think objectively before speaking. I'm keen to ensure that we don't fall out during this investigation. Deal?"

He shrugged. "I suppose."

"That's not good enough, Bob. I need more from you."

"All right. You have my word."

Sam studied Bob's face for a moment. The lines around his eyes were deeper than usual, and there was a heaviness in his voice that she hadn't noticed before. She knew this was personal for him, but she couldn't let that impede the investigation.

"There are two elements to the case that I find disturbing. Actually, make that three. The fire was set on purpose, after the murderer took Helen's life, obviously; it was set with the intention of covering up her murder. We also have to consider that the neighbours have overheard the couple arguing recently. We can't dismiss those facts, Bob. If Jason was under stress, if their marriage was falling apart, we can't ignore that."

Bob's jaw tightened, and then he heaved out a sigh. "I know I'm repeating myself, but bloody hell, Sam, raised voices don't necessarily mean that someone has it in for their spouse, does it? Shit happens, every marriage goes through rough patches."

"I know that." She ran a hand through her hair and caught a knot. "Ouch, that hurt. But I can't help thinking there's more to this, Bob. Call it gut instinct, if you want to. What you need to do is get over the fact that Jason is a good friend of yours."

"Yeah, so you said." Bob sighed again and rubbed at his chin. "I just don't want to see him dragged through the mud if he's innocent. That's all."

Sam's anger decreased. She understood where he was coming from, but her gut told her there was more to Jason than Bob was willing to see. "We'll be fair," she promised. "But we have to look at every angle."

"But please, please, don't forget there was a stranger spotted in the neighbourhood."

"I won't, I swear. Just like any other investigation we've dealt with together over the years, we'll thoroughly delve into every clue or piece of evidence that comes our way. Now, we need to either distract Jason for the next ten minutes or urge him to leave the area."

Bob's brow furrowed. "Why?"

"Because Des is eager to get the body moved."

"Shit. Okay, leave it to me."

She patted him on the shoulder. "I knew you wouldn't let me down."

TEN MINUTES LATER, Sam stood by the front door and escorted Des and his team to the van. She glanced over at Bob, who needed to restrain a distraught Jason. Sam tried to shrug off the sense that the scene was staged. Although she didn't know Jason, and while she might be guilty of misjudging him, she couldn't get past the feeling that there was something more to this investigation than met the eye, and that Jason's involvement was the part stirring up her insides. She grappled with the idea of pulling him in for questioning but wondered if doing that at this time would be classed as insensitive.

"Penny for them," Des whispered in her ear, startling her.

"Just thinking the usual. Wondering in what order things should be done on this one."

"The sooner I can get the results back to you, the better, eh? Do you want to attend the PM?"

Ordinarily, Sam would make every excuse under the sun to avoid attending, but this case was different. She nodded. "Okay, why not? Let me get in touch with the team first and bring them up to date on what we have discovered so far. That'll give them the go-ahead to start doing the necessary research into the couple's backgrounds."

"I'll leave that with you. Can you do it en route?"

Sam peered over Des' shoulder at how her partner was doing

with Jason. "I'll get Bob to drive, once he's calmed down the husband."

"No easy task, judging by the way he's reacting. Ring me if there's a delay. I intend cutting her open as soon as we get back."

Sam snorted. "Has anyone ever told you that you have a way with words?"

"Umm... once or twice throughout my career. Sod what they think. People either take me as they find me, or they can fuck off."

"You get worse. We'll see you soon."

Des strode purposefully towards his van.

Sam dipped back inside the house to speak with the assessor. "We're going to start our investigation now. I'll give you one of my cards. If you could send your report through ASAP, I'd appreciate it."

"Don't worry, I will. I can't promise when it will be, though."

Sam raised an eyebrow, which was enough to make him shift his feet in discomfort. She left the house, saying farewell to the SOCO techs who had remained on site to complete their tasks. She approached Jason's vehicle. By this time, Bob had managed to get his friend back in the car. Sam tapped on the driver's window, and Jason lowered it.

"When will I be able to see her?"

"The post-mortem will be carried out shortly. I should think the pathologist will call you tomorrow."

"What? Why can't I see her before the pathologist carries out the post-mortem?"

"We have to follow procedures, I'm afraid. Why don't you leave now? The pathologist will contact you as soon as he's ready."

"And what are you going to do?"

"We're going to the lab to oversee the PM," Sam replied respectfully.

"I see, and what about the investigation? Whoever did this is still out there, up to who knows what."

"I'm about to instruct my team now, on the way to the lab. Don't worry, the investigation is in hand. I'm not in the habit of slipping up, especially at the beginning of a case."

Jason stared ahead at what was left of his house and offered an apology. "I didn't mean to sound disrespectful. Bob here has been singing your praises for the past ten minutes."

"Thanks, partner. We make a great team. We will get to the bottom of how the fire started, I assure you. When was the exact time you spoke to your wife?"

His eyes narrowed as he contemplated the question. "Just before dinner last night. I didn't really check the time, maybe around sevenish."

"Did you eat at the hotel?"

He nodded and replied quietly, "Yes."

The way he was avoiding looking at her raised her suspicions again. "Were you alone?"

He coughed to clear his throat. "No, I was with an associate."

Sam gestured for Bob to write the information down. "We'll need his name." She scrutinised the way his hands twisted around the steering wheel.

"It was a woman. Why do you need her name? Oh, I see, to check my alibi because you're still keen to pin this on me, aren't you?"

"Not necessarily, but yes, we're going to need to check your alibi. Again, it's procedure. Please don't read anything into it."

He unplugged his phone that was on charge and tapped in his passcode. Then he showed the contact number to Bob so he could jot it down. "There you go. Will you have to tell her why you're calling her?"

"Do you see an issue with that?" Sam asked.

"No... I mean, yes. Oh, I don't know." He scratched his temple and then rested his head on the steering wheel.

Another move that raised an alarm bell within Sam. "Are you okay?"

He sat upright and stared at her. "Would you be if you'd lost your spouse in a fire?"

"Umm... we're just doing our job, mate," Bob interrupted before Sam could reveal the truth about losing her estranged husband in a fire after he'd poured petrol over himself, taking her fiancé's dog with him during the incident.

Sam shifted uncomfortably under his intense gaze. "As my partner stated, we're just doing our job."

"Well, I'm innocent. That's all you need to know. I suggest you move on and try to find the person who has destroyed my home and killed my wife because, as far as I'm concerned, I left my home in proper working order before I travelled to Carlisle."

"If you insist. We'll attend the PM now and let you get off. No doubt we'll be in touch soon if we have any further questions for you."

Jason ignored Sam and fist-bumped Bob. "Do your best for me, Bob. I'm relying on you."

"Don't worry, *we will.*"

Jason started the car and backed out of his spot. "We'll see," he shouted as he drove off.

"That went well," Sam said. She walked back to the vehicle and threw Bob the keys. "You can drive. I need to organise the team."

"Your wish is my command. Are you going to go easy on Jason?"

Sam chewed her lip. "We've been through this a couple of times already, Bob. Just because he's a friend, it doesn't mean we have to take our foot off the pedal."

Bob groaned and jumped into the driver's seat. He cursed after knocking his knees on the steering wheel and shot his seat back to give his legs more room. "Why are women so short?"

"Great things come in small packages. Didn't your father ever tell you that?"

"Nope. And for your information, my mother is five-eight."

"Wow, good for her. The average height of a woman in the UK is five-five. That's what I read in an article last week."

"So, what happened in your case?"

Sam got in beside him and slapped his arm. "Cheeky git. Make yourself useful and get us to the lab swiftly, without breaking the speed limit."

He grinned. "You're going to regret saying that."

He sped away, and she jolted forward in her seat. "Pack it in, or I'll take over and kick you out." She removed her phone from her pocket and rang the station. "Claire, it's me. We're on our way to the lab to oversee the PM. I wanted to check in with you, make sure everyone had a job to do back there."

"Hi, boss. We're going through what needs to be done now. Thought we'd better make a start while you were at the scene."

"I had a feeling you'd have it all in hand. Can you carry out the necessary checks on Jason and Helen Flintoff? Damn, I forgot to ask what Helen did for a living. Do you know, Bob?"

He shrugged. "I haven't got the foggiest."

"I heard," Claire said. "Don't worry, I'll see what I can find through her social media accounts. Anything in particular we should be looking at?"

"The usual. The husband was staying at a hotel in Carlisle, the Crest Hotel, wasn't it, Bob?"

"I think you're right," Bob confirmed.

"He was on a course. Apparently, he left home two days ago to attend the course. We haven't really gathered much information about the couple, except that the neighbours reported them arguing recently. Oh, and Jason is Bob's good friend."

"Oh heck, sorry to hear that, Bob," Claire said, via the speaker.

"Thanks, Claire," Bob replied. "Let's do what we can for Jason, eh? Go the extra mile on this one, if we can."

"Of course. Is there anything else, boss?" Claire asked.

"I don't think so. We'll return to the station once the PM is over."

"We'll get cracking on it now. Good luck."

Sam ended the call. "Did Jason tell you where he was going?"

"No, I tried to persuade him to visit a mutual friend of ours, but he said he'd prefer to be alone."

"I can understand that. Maybe he'll stay in a hotel for a few days then. Where does he work?"

"At a large accountancy firm in Workington. I know where it is but can't remember its name for the life of me."

"Don't worry about it. How well do you know each other?"

"Well enough," Bob retorted sharply.

"Why are you being so defensive about this?"

"I'm not. Put yourself in my shoes. How would you react if one of your best friends had just lost everything?"

Sam raised her hands. "All right, point taken. I have a feeling we're going to have a frustrating time ahead of us. I need you to remember not to take things personally during the investigation. You're going to have to remain impartial at all times."

"I hear you. How many more times are you going to tell me that?"

"Sorry for repeating myself." She sensed she would need to tread carefully during the investigation for fear of upsetting Bob, something she wasn't looking forward to.

The rest of the brief journey was carried out in silence.

2

When they arrived at the mortuary, a tech showed them to the changing room. "You know where the theatre is, don't you, Inspector?" he asked.

"I do. Down the corridor, the last room on the right."

"That's correct. I'll leave you to it. Feel free to use the lockers to put your personal possessions in, if you have any."

"Thanks."

The young man nodded and left the room.

"I hate having to attend these damn things," Bob complained.

Sam slipped on the green top and trousers and then pulled on the half-wellies, as she called them. "You don't have to go through this if you don't want to. The choice is yours, Bob."

"Too late now. I'm suited and booted. Might as well get it over and done with."

They left the changing room and joined Des in the theatre. His assistant was on hand and arranging the equipment on the trolley beside him. The victim's charred body lay naked on the table. It was patchy, after her clothes had been removed.

"Are you okay?" Sam whispered to Bob.

"Don't start checking in on me every five minutes. You're only going to tick me off."

"Pardon me for caring. If you want to leave at any time, I wouldn't mind, just go."

"Thanks. I'll be all right. Stop fussing."

"Everything all right?" Des asked, his gaze flicking warily between Sam and Bob.

"Yes. We're both fine, aren't we, partner?"

"For the umpteenth time today, everything is fine and dandy. Can we get on with this?"

"I was about to suggest the same." Des held out his hand, and his assistant gave him the scalpel. He concentrated as he made the Y-incision.

Sam sensed Bob tense up beside her, and he gulped when Des pulled back the skin to reveal the internal organs. Des ran through the procedure for the recording, pointing out that the victim had several wounds on the front of her skull, presumably from a hammer, which he'd already told them at the crime scene. He did offer something new, though, when he opened up the lungs.

"No smoke in the lungs, which means she died before the fire."

"Thanks for the confirmation. So, as suspected, the fire was probably started to cover up the fact that Helen had already been killed," Sam proposed.

"I think your suspicion is correct, Sam." He concentrated his efforts for the next ten minutes on taking samples from each of her organs but paused a little while later.

"Is something wrong?" Sam asked. She shuffled closer to the body to get a better view.

"She was pregnant."

"What?" Bob asked. "Jason didn't tell us that."

Sam glanced at her partner and shrugged. "Perhaps he didn't know. Can you tell how far gone she was, Des?"

"It would only be a guess, maybe two to three months, no more than that."

"Is there a possibility that she didn't even know?" Sam asked.

"Maybe you're right, Sam."

Sam's mind raced. "Shit, could that be why she was killed?"

"What are you talking about?" Bob asked, perplexed.

"Ignore me. My mind is picking through the pieces, searching for a motive as to why someone would want to kill her."

"What if she was having an affair?" Des suggested.

Sam nodded. "It would explain why the couple had been heard arguing lately."

"Come on, seriously?" Bob asked. "No way. They loved each other."

"You can't say that for certain, Bob. You told me you barely knew the woman," Sam countered.

"I know Jason, though, and he was besotted with his wife."

Sam sensed the conversation was about to take a turn for the worse, so she backed down.

After studying Sam and Bob for a few seconds, Des said, "Should you be here, Bob?"

"We've discussed that. Bob said he would prefer to be here," Sam jumped in quickly.

"The decision is yours, of course. But during the examination, I'm going to be saying things that probably won't sit well with you, Bob. You need to prepare yourself for that."

"I'm prepared. Stop worrying about me."

Des' gaze dropped on Sam, and she nodded for him to continue.

ONCE THE PM WAS COMPLETED, with no other shocks uncovered, Sam and Bob returned to the station.

"Do you want to stop off somewhere and have a drink first?" she asked.

"No, I'm not allowed to drink alcohol on duty."

She smiled. "I meant a coffee. However, if you needed a drink, I'm sure no one would mind in the circumstances."

"Not needed. I just want to get on with the investigation, Sam."

"Okay. I'm here if you need to talk, you know that."

"I do. I'm fine. Just processing everything right now."

"Umm... please don't share the news with Jason, not yet. Let's sit on the information for a few days first."

"I agree. He's going to be devastated when he finds out."

"Did they want kids?" Sam asked. She pulled into the outside lane of the roundabout and drove towards the station, which was five minutes away.

"I'm not sure. The topic was never raised, not from what I can remember."

"What type of parents do you think they would have made?"

"Hard to say. I don't think anyone can really say that until they have to deal with a baby of their own. The sleepless nights, the constant crying, unsure of what's going on with the little one. It's a tough job at the best of times, for both parents. I can't believe she was pregnant and he didn't know."

"You can't speculate about that, Bob. Like I said, if they knew, maybe that was the source of the arguments. I'm intrigued to hear what Jason has to say about that, if anything."

"I think it's too soon to ask him."

"We'll monitor the situation. Let's see what the rest of the team has uncovered and go from there."

Sam drew into her parking space at the station. She locked the car and watched her partner walk towards the main entrance, his shoulders slumped and his head down. It didn't bode well for what lay ahead of them. She would need to keep a close eye on him for the rest of the day.

Bob made them both a drink while Sam did the rounds with the team.

"Have you discovered anything while we've been out?" She crossed the room to see what Claire had for her first.

"I've searched the SM accounts for both of them. Yesterday, Helen was at a bridal fair down at Muncaster Castle."

Sam's mouth dropped open. The comment had shocked her to the core. Regaining her composure, she asked, "Why? If she was already married? By the way, I was there with my sister."

"Oh no. Gosh, yes, you mentioned you were taking the day off to go somewhere. I didn't put two and two together. Helen was the one who organised the event."

Sam frowned. "Did she work at the castle?"

"No, she was an events' manager for Spark and Shine Events here in Workington."

"Can you show me a photo of her?"

Claire angled her screen in Sam's direction.

"Oh shit. I had a bloody conversation with her yesterday." Sam perched on the desk behind her as her legs wobbled.

Bob handed her a mug. "Everything okay?"

"No. I met Helen yesterday at the bridal fair I attended."

"I don't understand. Why was she there? She's already married."

"She was the one who organised the event. My sister had a stall there. I helped her set up and then circulated the room, getting ideas for my wedding. We stumbled across each other a few times during the day. She came across as being really friendly. Damn, I'm shocked. Shit, I need to tell my sister." She took her mug and ran into the office to make the call.

"Hi, Crystal. Can you talk?"

"I can. What's up, sis? You sound harassed."

"Umm... I have some news for you. Are you sitting down?"

"Oh Christ, it's not Dad, is it?"

"No, no, no. Sorry for putting the fear of God into you. Listen, when we went to Muncaster yesterday, you seemed really friendly with Helen, the woman who organised the event. How do you know her?"

"I don't, not really. She's arranged a few events like that in the past that I've attended, and we just formed a friendship. I noticed you talking with her a few times throughout the day. She's nice, isn't she? Why are you asking? She isn't hounding you, is she?"

"No, it's nothing like that. Sorry, sweetheart, I have some bad news for you."

"Bugger. What's that, Sam?"

"Helen was found murdered this morning."

Her sister gasped, and then silence filled the line, prompting Sam to question if her sister was all right.

"Yes, yes, I'm still here. Oh my God, I wasn't expecting you to say that, Sam. Murdered? How do you know? Or is that a stupid question?"

"We were called to attend a fire this morning. She lived in a cottage. It was destroyed in the fire, and Helen was found inside."

"So the fire killed her? Is that what you're telling me? Oh God, this is awful news. She was such a wonderful lady; she really cared about the exhibitors and tried to help us gain more attention for our stands. She always offered constructive criticism that we all took on board. Sorry, I'm going on and not allowing you to answer my question."

"It's all right. No, the fire didn't kill her. We believe she answered her front door, and someone struck her with a heavy object."

"What the fuck? God, that's terrible, Sam. Who would do such a thing?"

"That's what we need to find out. I wanted you to hear the news before it broke on the TV and radio. There were a few reporters at the scene."

"Callous bastards, always on the lookout for a juicy story, intent on ripping a family apart. Actually, I was listening to the news earlier, and they mentioned something about a fire. I was busy doing my accounts, and the rest of the story went over my head."

"So, they didn't mention her name then?"

"I can't answer that, sorry. Was anyone else hurt in the fire?"

"No, her husband was away on a course yesterday. He arrived while we were at the scene."

"Shit. I bet that went down well, not. How did he take the news, or is that another dumb question?"

"He's shocked, of course." Sam stopped short of telling her that she was a tad suspicious of Jason Flintoff. "Turns out that he's one of my partner's best friends."

"Oh, my goodness. What a dreadful situation to find yourselves in. Is Bob okay? Will he be able to continue working on the case?"

"He's a bit numb at the moment. Hopefully, he'll pull himself together soon. We've just attended the PM."

"No, you didn't make him go through that, did you?"

"I gave him the option to walk away, but he chose to be there. Umm... this needs to remain between you and me."

"What? You know I never blab about anything you tell me."

"During the PM, the pathologist told us that Helen was pregnant."

Her sister gasped again and started sobbing.

"Oh, Crystal, I'm sorry, I shouldn't have told you."

"Life is so unfair. That poor baby," Crystal said between sniffles.

The bell rang in the shop.

"You'd better dry your eyes and see who that is, love. Take care. I'll call you later."

"Thanks for confiding in me, Sam. Please, please do your best to find the person responsible for her murder."

"That goes without saying. Chin up. I love you."

"Love you back."

Sam ended the call and crossed the room with her mug to look at the views of the hills in the distance. *What I wouldn't give to be out there hiking the hills right now.*

A knock on the door interrupted her thoughts. She turned to see Bob poking his head around the door.

"Just checking you're okay, are you?"

"I'm fine. I broke the news to my sister."

"Did Crystal know Helen well?"

"Only through the events they had met at over the years. She told me Helen was a wonderful woman, very friendly and helpful to the exhibitors."

"I'm still having trouble processing it, Sam. None of it is making any sense to me."

Sam shook her head. "Nor me. Let's ensure we dot all the I's on this one, mate, eh?"

"Absolutely."

Sam tapped a finger on her cheek as she thought. "What about requesting CCTV footage from the castle?"

"What are you thinking? Does the event have something to do with her murder?"

Sam shrugged. "Hard to say. I think we need to cover all the angles open to us, and quickly. Can you arrange that for me while I have a word with the rest of the team to see what other information they have gathered for us?"

"I'll get on to them now."

He left the room. Sam downed the rest of her coffee and then joined the team. Liam and Oliver were sitting together at Liam's desk.

"This looks like a hive of activity. What have you got, gents?"

"We're going over the couple's finances. Haven't found anything out of the ordinary yet, boss."

"That's a good sign. It could prove vital as things progress."

She went back to Claire to see if she had discovered anything useful via the SM accounts. "My sister was shocked to hear the news. According to Crystal, Helen usually went out of her way to help the stallholders at the events. I remember chatting with her, and she had a friendly manner. Such a shame she's no longer with us. Anything interesting showing up here?"

"She was pretty active on Facebook and Instagram, not so much on the other platforms. I've made a list of her friends. She had over five hundred. I went back over the past six months, listing only the friends who had either liked or commented on her posts."

"And you've whittled it down to how many?"

"Around ten. She also has a sister, Davina."

"Ah, right, okay. That might be worth a shot, speaking with her. Any other family members mentioned?"

"Her mother and father are both active on FB, at least they seem to be. Matthew and Linda Baldwin."

"Can you get an address for them? I think that should be our next call, just in case Jason hasn't told them yet."

"Let me do some digging for you—just two seconds."

Sam squeezed Claire's shoulder and drifted around the room to check how Bob was getting on. He was waiting on the phone. He raised a finger when someone answered.

"Ah, yes, this is DS Bob Jones from the Cumbria Constabulary..."

Sam sat at the desk beside him and listened to him while pretending she was scrolling through her phone. She was pleased he handled the call well, dispersing the thoughts she had of him not being a hundred percent in the game.

Bob ended the call. "They've agreed to send us the disc. I suppose we could have sent someone down there to pick it up. I never thought about it."

"It's fine. If they post it today, we should receive it either tomorrow or the next day." Sam considered the options open to them again and shook her head. "That's not good enough. I'm determined to hit this investigation on all fronts. Bob, can you ring them back? Tell them that we'll send someone to pick up the disc."

Bob frowned. "Okay. If that's what you want me to do."

Sam grinned. "I do." She faced Oliver and Liam, and, still grinning, she asked, "Do you boys fancy a trip down to Muncaster?"

They faced each other and nodded.

"I'm up for it if you are?" Liam said.

"Good. One of you can still work from the car while the other drives."

"Consider it done, boss," Oliver replied. He stood and removed his jacket from the back of his chair. "I'll drive."

"Okay, you get on the road, and we'll do the same. Keep in touch with Claire about the research en route. Try to question the staff while you're there. Ask if they saw anything suspicious going on."

Oliver and Liam left the office.

"I'll ring the castle again to let them know the boys are on the way," Bob said.

3

The detached house appeared to be newly built but wasn't part of an estate. Instead, it was surrounded by land, a few miles north of Bridgefoot.

Bob whistled. "Wow, this is impressive."

"You're telling me. Set in a stunning location as well. What's not to love? Do you know them?"

"Not as such. I've met them once or twice at family barbecues, but I don't think I've ever held a serious conversation with them. Unlike Jason's family; that's a different matter, only because I've known him for years."

"There are two cars on the drive. Hopefully, they're both at home."

"It'll make life easier if they are," Bob replied.

"I'm going to park on the road."

"Can I ask why?"

Sam shrugged. "I feel it would be less of an intrusion. Why don't you jump out? Then I can pull in tighter to the hedge."

Bob hopped out of the car. Sam joined him a little while later and looked back at her achievement.

He smirked. "Are you seeking praise?"

"No. Piss off. Come on, let's get this over with."

"Yeah, I can't say I'm looking forward to this chore."

"That makes two of us." Sam entered the large gate and closed it behind them. The gravel crunched under their feet.

A woman appeared in the bay window of a downstairs room. She called out, presumably to her husband, that they had visitors. The door opened before Sam had a chance to ring the bell. She was prepared and showed the man her warrant card.

"Hello, Mr Baldwin. I'm DI Sam Cobbs, and this is my partner, DS Bob Jones. Would it be possible to come and speak with you and your wife?"

His brow wrinkled, and his gaze shifted from Sam to Bob and back to Sam again. "May I ask why? What your visit is concerning?"

"It's a personal matter, sir."

He raised an eyebrow but didn't challenge her. Instead, he took a step back, allowing them to enter the hallway.

"You have a beautiful home. Have you lived here long?"

"A few months. We built it ourselves, well, not with our own hands. We employed builders to construct our dream home, and this is the result."

"It's exceptional."

"Thank you. I take it you haven't come all this way to praise our efforts. What's this about, Inspector?"

"Maybe you can introduce us to your wife first, and then I'll explain."

"Very well. Come through to the lounge."

They followed him into the first room off the hallway. It was very grand, with bespoke bookcases in both alcoves on either side of the impressive fireplace, which housed a substantial wood-burning stove. The furnishings were a muted palette, and the curtains were a royal blue, the only pop of colour in the room.

"Linda, these two people are police officers."

"What? Why are you here?"

Mr Baldwin moved closer and wrapped his arm around his wife. "They've yet to tell me. Do you want to take a seat?"

"Thank you. I think it would be wise," Sam replied.

Bob removed his notebook from his pocket before he sat on the sofa next to Sam. The Baldwins sat opposite, Linda in the easy chair and Matthew on the arm. The couple held hands. Mrs Baldwin appeared to be visibly upset, as if expecting bad news.

"Thank you for agreeing to see us. I need to ask if either of you has spoken with Jason yet?"

The couple glanced at each other and then shook their heads.

"Not recently," Matthew said. "Why?"

"Umm... this morning, we were called to Jason and Helen's house."

"What? Why?" Matthew demanded.

"Hush now. Let the inspector speak, Matt."

"I apologise. Go on. What do you mean you were called to their house?"

Sam inhaled a breath to calm her nerves. "We responded to a report of a fire taking place at the property."

"A fire? Oh my... that's strange, Helen hasn't rung us. Was anyone hurt in the blaze? Was the fire small or large?" Linda asked. She gripped her husband's hand tighter.

"It was a significant fire that destroyed the property. I'm sorry to be the bearer of bad news, but I'm afraid your daughter died in the fire."

Matthew leapt off the chair and ran a hand through his short, grey hair. "She what? You can't come in here and tell us that our daughter is dead."

Sam could tell Linda was in shock. Tears bulged in her eyes, and her mouth gaped open. She reached out a hand for her husband.

He ignored her and continued his rant at Sam. "Why weren't we told right away? And where was he? Did he die in the fire as well?"

"If you mean her husband, Jason, no, he was away on a course. A friend rang him. He turned up at the house a few hours later. He's mortified to have lost his wife."

"And you expect me to believe that? Why didn't he call us? No, forget I asked. We've never seen eye to eye."

"Can I ask why?" Sam asked, intrigued.

"I've never felt he was good enough for my daughter."

Sam sensed Bob stiffen next to her. *Don't you dare react, Bob. Just keep taking notes and keep your mouth shut.* "Is there a particular reason why you would think that? From what we've gathered so far, they're both professional people who had a good marriage."

"Who told you that?" he asked.

"We've spoken to some of the neighbours, and one of Jason's good friends corroborated the fact."

Matthew paced the floor, ignoring his wife's outstretched hand.

His wife sobbed, and still he continued to rant and pace the floor. "This is unbelievable. We should have been told before this."

Linda finally found her voice. "Matt, stop it! Sit down, you're making me angry and upsetting me even more."

Sam watched the interaction between the husband and wife. She believed there was a lot of love there, but something appeared to be strained at the same time.

Matt finally relented. He sat in the same spot and put an arm around his wife's shoulders whilst he ran his free hand around the back of his neck. "I can't believe she's gone. The apple of our eye."

"One of them," his wife corrected.

"Yes, sorry."

"I take it you have other children," Sam said, despite knowing that Helen had a sister called Davina.

"Yes, we have another daughter. She's younger than Helen and is called Davina. Oh no, she'll be devastated to hear of her sister's passing," Linda replied.

"Would you like me to tell her?" Sam asked.

"No!" Matt shouted. "That's our job to tell her. How did it start? The fire?"

"Does it matter?" his wife screeched. "She's dead. That's all we need to know."

"Actually, there is more to the story," Sam told the couple.

"What more could there be?" Matt demanded. His eyes narrowed as he stared at Sam.

"We've just come from overseeing the post-mortem. While we're waiting for the pathologist to send his report through, he confirmed that your daughter was attacked before she died."

"Attacked? How? And by whom?" Linda said. She reached for her husband's hand again, which was draped over her shoulder.

"It would seem that Helen opened the front door to someone. The pathologist believes your daughter was attacked with an object and was likely to have been dead before the fire was started."

"What the bloody hell... Who would do such a thing?" Matt asked. "What aren't you telling us? I'm sensing you're not giving us the full story, Inspector."

Sam shrugged. "I'm sorry, with regard to how your daughter died, that's all we know at this time. During the post-mortem, the pathologist checked the lungs. There was no sign of smoke inhalation, therefore, in his expert opinion, Helen died from her wounds before..."

"And someone started the fire to cover the fact that she was already dead. Is that what you're telling us?" Matt asked.

"So it would seem. I have to ask, did Helen ever mention that she was in any kind of trouble?"

"Trouble? No, never. She was a bright young woman. Career-driven, she lived and breathed her job. And if anyone tells you otherwise, they're liars. Isn't that right, Linda?"

"Yes. She rang me the other day, told me how excited she was to be organising the bridal fair at Muncaster Castle, and even asked me to go with her. I would have gone, too, but the timing was off as we both had appointments at the hospital eye clinic. You can't put those types of appointments off. You never know when you're likely to get a new one."

"So, she was excited about the fair?"

"Yes. Bridal fairs were her favourite events to organise."

"I attended the fair as I'm getting married in the summer. I spoke to Helen at the event."

"You did?" Linda said, a smile lighting up her face. "I bet she made you feel comfortable in your surroundings, didn't she?"

"Yes. My sister owns a bridal boutique in Workington. She was the one who introduced us. Crystal had dealt with Helen several times over the years."

"I think I know your sister. My niece is getting married soon, and Helen recommended Crystal's boutique to my sister. She has so many beautiful gowns to choose from."

"She has. My sister researches very carefully to bring the best designs to the town," Sam announced proudly before mentally kicking herself in the shin. "Sorry, this isn't helping. Going back to Helen, did she usually confide in you?"

Linda glanced sideways when her husband faced her.

"Linda and Helen were always having secret chats in the kitchen, which usually stopped when I entered the room."

"Nonsense, don't listen to him. He's got a big birthday coming up soon. Helen and I were trying to organise something different for him for a change."

"Oh, no. I didn't even think about that. I'm sorry, love. I know all the secrecy has caused some tension between us lately."

"You should trust me more, Matt," Linda was quick to add.

"Did Helen mention anything about her marriage?"

"No, why?" Matt asked. "It's barely been five minutes since you told me that their marriage was solid. So why ask us if their marriage was okay?"

"I was less than truthful with you… one of their neighbours mentioned that she'd overheard them arguing recently."

"There you go. I knew he couldn't be trusted," Matt said. He folded his arms and leaned back. "What did I tell you? I knew everything wasn't rosy in that house. I wouldn't trust him as far as I could throw him."

"Matt, shut up. Unless you have anything concrete to share with the inspector, no one wants to know how you feel about Jason. In my opinion, he's always looked after Helen well."

"What are you saying? That I'm not allowed to say what I think about him? You know as well as I do that I've never trusted him from the second I laid eyes on him."

Sam nudged her knee against Bob's, warning him not to react to

Matt's outburst. "Perhaps you can tell me what it is that is causing you to doubt Jason, Mr Baldwin?"

"I would if I could. There's just something off about him. I'm sure you must get that reaction from time to time when you meet someone, Inspector."

"Absolutely. I'm not doubting you, however, it would be good if you gave me an insight into what it is you don't trust about him. Has he ever given you any reason not to trust him?"

Matt bowed his head. "No. I can never put my finger on it. I'm begging you not to allow yourself to be hoodwinked by him, just because he's lost his wife, our daughter."

"Jason happens to be a good friend of mine," Bob jumped to Jason's defence.

Sam cringed. "Sergeant, there's no need to say more."

"No," Matt interjected, "let's have it, if you've got something to say. I knew I recognised you when you turned up on our doorstep."

"Yes, we've met a few times over the years. Jason is very cut up about Helen's death."

"So cut up, he neglected to inform her parents that she had passed away?" Matt challenged.

"Umm... I'm sorry about that, but if you don't get on, then why would he come here and tell you?"

Matt's eyes widened, and he leaned forward. "Maybe because it would have been the right thing to do. What do you think?"

Sam raised a hand between the warring males. "Please, this isn't getting us anywhere."

Matt pointed at Bob. "He shouldn't be on the case. Either he's removed at once, or I'll put in a complaint."

"Don't be so ridiculous, Matt," his wife reprimanded him and lowered the offending finger. "Don't make this worse than it already is. It's been clear for years that you can't stand Jason. Don't let that fact cloud your judgement. So what if the sergeant is a friend of his? He's a professional police officer, and they have rules in place, preventing him from taking sides during an investigation, isn't that right, Inspector?"

"Absolutely. I can vouch for my partner's professionalism. If I had any reservations about his abilities during this investigation, I would have assigned him to work on another case. I haven't. He's lived in this area all his life and went to school with a large number of the population of Workington. There are bound to be certain cases he'll work on throughout his career where he knows either the victim or their partner personally. I can assure you, he will give this investigation a hundred percent every day. He'll have me to deal with if he doesn't," she added with a smile aimed at her partner.

"The inspector is right. I could have hidden the fact that Jason is one of my closest friends from the outset. I didn't. I revealed the truth immediately. I'm as eager as Inspector Cobbs is to solve this crime. If anything, knowing the victim and Jason as well as I do should make me more determined to find the person responsible."

Sam nodded her agreement.

"Don't listen to my husband. I'm happy for you to continue on the case, Sergeant," Linda said. "Stop putting unnecessary obstacles in their way, Matt, or you and I are going to fall out. Am I making myself clear here?"

"Yes, dear."

"Now apologise to the sergeant."

Matt rolled his eyes and then said, "I'm sorry. Please forgive me. The news you came here to deliver has shocked me to the core."

"I understand. There's no need for you to apologise," Bob told him. "I swear, if Jason has anything to hide, I will get to the truth. I have seen no signs of that so far. Have you, Inspector?"

Shit! Thanks for putting me on the spot, pal. "Not yet. We've only met briefly. I will be interviewing him in a few days once he's got over the shock."

"And yet here you are, questioning us about our daughter and her marriage. Why are you giving him preferential treatment?" Matt asked.

Sam shook her head. "I'm not. I didn't feel it was appropriate to question him at this time. My priority was coming here to see you to ensure you heard the news directly rather than learning about your daughter's death via the media. There were quite a few reporters at the scene this morning."

"Thank you. We really appreciate your thoughtfulness," Linda said. "Can we see our daughter?"

Matt's head whipped around, and he shouted, "No, we can't see her like that. If she died in the fire, she's going to be burnt. Why would you want to remember her like that, Linda? Don't punish yourself even more than you have to."

Sam nodded. "I think your husband is right, Mrs Baldwin. At least think about it before making an appointment."

Linda broke down and pulled her hand away from her husband's. "But I want to say goodbye to her. I don't care what she looks like."

"Why don't you give the pathologist a call? He's good at offering advice to family members in cases such as this," Sam said.

"I think that's an excellent idea, darling. We'll give him a call later. Do you have his number?"

Sam scrolled through her phone and asked Bob to jot down the lab's number rather than hand out Des's mobile information, aware of how irate he would be if he found out. Bob tore out the sheet of paper and handed it to Matthew Baldwin.

"Thank you. Is there anything you need from us?" Matthew asked.

"I don't think so. No, wait, would it be possible for you to give us Davina's address and phone number, please?"

"Why do you want to speak with her?" Linda asked, then blew her nose into a tissue.

"It's procedure. We always check in with other close family members during an investigation. Does she live locally?"

"Yes, in Workington, not far from the station, actually," Linda replied. "If you give me your notebook, I can write her details down for you."

Bob passed Linda his notebook.

"Matt, can you get my phone? It's in the kitchen on the side. I can never remember her number."

Her husband left the room.

Linda leaned in and whispered, "I'm sorry if you felt he was over the top about you being friends with Jason."

Bob waved his hand. "It's forgotten about. I promise not to let it cloud my judgement."

With that, Matt returned to the room and eyed them all suspiciously. "I bet my name has been mud in here during my absence," he grumbled as he handed his wife her phone.

"Get over yourself. The universe doesn't revolve around you, Matt."

"Charming. I was only speaking my mind."

"It's forgotten about," Bob assured him.

"Good, I'd hate to offend you and give you a reason to take your foot off the gas. I want to know the ins and outs of what happened to my daughter and why someone would want to kill her. That sounds shocking, saying it out loud like that."

"One last question before we leave," Sam said.

"What's that?" Matthew asked.

"Do you know of any reason why someone would want to harm your daughter? Has she fallen out with anyone lately? What about an old boyfriend? Anyone in her past who has possibly threatened her over the years?"

The couple both stared at the carpet in front of them and shook their heads.

"No, not that I can think of," Linda said. "Matt, what about you?"

"I was about to say the same. She wasn't the type to fall out with people. She always bent over backwards to help everyone. I believe that's what made her so good at her job."

"I can understand that. She was very helpful to me at the bridal fair. Okay, I'm going to leave you one of my cards. If you should think of anything later that you believe might be helpful for the investigation, please get in touch." Sam handed the card to Mrs Baldwin and rose to her feet.

Bob flipped his notebook shut and also stood.

"I'll show you out," Matthew said.

"Please, Inspector. I'm begging you, do your best to find out who killed our daughter," Linda said, a sob catching in her throat.

Sam took a step towards her. "You have my word on that." She followed Matt and Bob out of the room.

"I'm sorry for going over the top in there. Hopefully, you'll understand in the circumstances."

Sam shook her head. "You don't have to apologise for saying what's on your mind, sir. I just wanted to assure you a second time that we're going to do everything in our power to find out how Helen died."

"And, I hope, punish the person who killed her."

"That goes without saying. Take care of each other. You're going to need to support your wife over the next few days."

"I know, she's not as strong as she makes out." He opened the door to let them out and closed it gently behind them.

Sam didn't say anything until they were back in the car. "Are you all right?"

"I'll survive. I don't blame them—or should I say him—for challenging me about being Jason's friend. I suppose I would do the same if I ever found myself in a similar situation. I stand by what I said back there, though. I can't see Jason being involved in this."

"I know. It's going to be up to us to figure out who the killer is, though. I'm going to check in with the team before heading off." She rang the station. "Claire, it's me. Stop looking for Davina. Her parents have given us her address and phone number. Have you heard from the boys?"

"Ah, okay. Not yet. I'm presuming they are on their way back now."

"I'll give them a call, then I'll ring Davina, ask if we can drop by and see her on the way back to the station."

"Sounds like a plan."

"See you soon." Sam ended the call and then rang Oliver's number. "Hey, it's me. How's it going at your end?"

"We're on our way, just passing Holmrook now, boss. We've got the disc."

"Brilliant. We've broken the news to the parents. I'm about to call their other daughter now, see if we can drop by and have a chat with her before we return to base."

"Okay. We'll get started on the disc when we get back."

"Great, thanks, Oliver." She ended the call and asked Bob for Davina's number.

He read it out to her, and she dialled the number, only for it to go to voicemail. "Hello, Davina. This is Detective Inspector Sam Cobbs from the Cumbria Constabulary. If you can call me back at your convenience, I'd appreciate it." She reeled off the number and then ended the call. "Oh well, we might as well return to the station and wait for her to get back to us."

"I suppose we should have asked the parents where she works. We could have visited her."

"Yeah, you're right, that was remiss of me. We'll see if she gets in touch with me later. If not, I'll call her parents."

IT WAS Sam's idea to stop off at the local baker's on the way back to the station. Loaded with goodies, she and Bob marched up the stairs to the incident room to find the rest of the team waiting for them. Bob made the coffee while she handed around the lunches.

"You can swap with each other if I've got the orders wrong. I don't think I have, though."

"Nope, spot on for me, thanks, boss," Liam said after checking his ham and tomato sandwich.

"Mine's great as well, thanks, boss," Oliver said, appreciating his chicken salad on white.

"You're welcome. Have you started going through the disc yet?"

"We have," Oliver confirmed. He set his lunch aside and showed her what they'd discovered. "I thought you might be interested in this part."

Sam leaned over his shoulder and viewed the footage. Helen was in the castle's hallway when someone called her name. At least, that's what it looked like to Sam. She watched on as Helen slowly turned towards the approaching man. "Hmm... he seems angry. Crap, I wish there was sound available."

"That's what we thought," Oliver said.

The conversation appeared to get heated between Helen and this man. It lasted around five minutes before Helen threw her arm out as if to dismiss the man. Another bloke appeared at the end of the hallway. Helen briefly conversed with him and followed him back through the large door at the end, leaving the fella she'd had words with seething. He kicked out at a nearby chair, venting his anger.

"Very interesting. Keep scrolling through the footage. Have you got other angles? Different areas? Or is there only one camera up there?"

"We've got access to several different cameras on here. We'll keep scrolling through it, see if anything else comes to light."

"I wonder if he was an exhibitor. Maybe he was complaining about where his stall was positioned," Sam said. "Let me know what you find. Hold on, rewind it and let me take a photo. I can send it to my sister, ask her if she knows the man."

"That's a great idea," Bob said. He arrived with the drinks and handed them around.

Oliver rewound the disc and cleared up the image to the best of his abilities before Sam took a still shot of the man.

"Great, thanks, Oliver. I'll have my lunch in the office. I can have a natter with my sister if she's not too busy."

"All right for some," Bob grumbled and handed Sam her coffee.

"Grumpy old git. Enjoy the lunch I bought you."

He rolled his eyes to the ceiling and grinned.

Sam took her lunch and coffee through to the office and rang her sister. "Are you busy?"

"Oh, hi. I was just thinking about you. No, I've put the Closed sign up on the door while I have a quick sandwich. How's it going?"

"Snap. Umm... my team is going through the footage from the bridal fair, and something interesting has caught our attention. If I send a photo of a man over to you, can you tell me if you know him?"

"Sure, send it over."

"Doing it now." She pressed the Send button. "We're not sure if he works at the castle or if he was an exhibitor. Do you know him?"

"Let me have a peek." Her sister paused as she viewed the photo and then came back on the line. "Nope, I don't recognise him."

"I know the picture isn't the best. Can you study it again? It's really important."

"No, sorry, Sam. Why are you so interested in this bloke?"

"We caught him arguing with Helen in the hallway."

"What the fuck? And you think he's the killer."

"Hey, let's not jump to conclusions. It's caught our interest. I'm not labelling the man as her killer, not yet."

"Oh, my mistake, sorry. I'd be crap at being a police officer. Everyone would be suspicious in my eyes. Talking of which, have you heard from the black sheep of the family lately?"

"God, shamefully, I haven't thought about Mike in ages. No, have you?"

Sam's thoughts drifted to the day they'd all showed up at court to support her brother, and he turned on them all, her sister and parents included, for not being there for him. Mike had got into taking drugs in his late teens. His parents had been the first to turn their backs on him, whereas Crystal and Sam had always been there for him. That was until he'd killed an old man in the post office he'd robbed to buy drugs. Although their relationship had soured that day, Sam had persuaded her parents and sister to attend her brother's hearing to lend him support during his trial. But Mike had shown himself and his family up. He'd shouted that he was a victim of circumstances and that his parents had never truly loved him. He blamed them for going off the rails. That episode had destroyed her parents. Sam's father had sworn blind that he would never speak to or see their brother again. And when their mother had passed away, her father warned Crystal and Sam not to tell Mike because he didn't want a con at the funeral.

That had gone against the grain for Sam, but she cherished her father and decided to abide by his wishes. Crystal was always the first to raise the subject of Mike.

"Hey, are you still there?" Crystal asked.

"Sorry, I was lost in a world of my own for a second or two. I often wonder how he's getting on. He'll be off the drugs by now."

"You reckon? The last documentary I saw about the prison service stated that drugs are rife inside and they're struggling to get a handle on the problem."

"It's bound to be, the number of drug-related crimes that happen in our society today."

"Shocking, isn't it? Surely these people know what it does to the brain. Do they like going around in a daze all the time? I get a dodgy headache, and that's me tucked up in bed for the day. Nothing else matters except ridding myself of that dreadful feeling of light-headedness."

"I can't answer that. I've never been inclined to take them. People need to realise that putting foreign substances into their body is bound to have a devastating effect on how their body functions. That's my tuppence worth. Oh God, I hope you haven't tempted fate by bringing his name up."

"Sorry, I should have thought about that before I mentioned him. Just ignore him if he decides to get in touch with you. We're all getting on with our lives. We didn't make him take drugs; that was his decision. You and I spent hour upon hour trying to talk sense into the bugger when he first started on them. He didn't want to know, and look where it got him in the end."

Sam sighed. This wasn't the way she'd imagined this conversation going. "Well, that's put a dampener on my day. I dread to think how I would react if he ever got in touch again."

"Yeah, me neither. I'd say the likelihood of him reaching out to either of us is pretty non-existent."

"I hope you're right. Anyway, getting back to the investigation, Bob and I have just come back from sharing the news about Helen with her parents."

"Oh heck. I bet that was a dreadful conversation to hold. What about her husband? Didn't he tell them?"

"No. I thought he might have reached out to them, but sadly, that wasn't the case."

"What a terrible situation. I still can't believe she's dead. She was so full of life at the bridal fair, ensuring everyone was set up and ready to serve the customers…" Her voice trailed off, and she sniffled.

"Are you all right?"

"I will be. Just goes to prove that you have to make sure you enjoy life every day because you never know what's around the corner, do you?"

"Yep, you've got that right. What happened to Chris is a prime example of that."

"He was a prat. I bet he couldn't live with the guilt of cheating on you, and when his floozy kicked him out and he found out that you had moved on, he regretted his actions and couldn't deal with either the guilt or shame."

Sam's mind drifted back again to the fateful day her husband, as he still was at the time, had set fire to himself. She shook her head to rid herself of the images.

"Sam? Sorry, are you okay? I shouldn't have brought the past up. What's done is done."

"I still think about him now and again."

"You're bound to. You were with each other for nearly ten years. You need to take comfort in the fact that you have a good man beside you now."

"I know. I count my blessings that he's still with me, too. It was touch and go after that knife attack."

"He's a fighter. Don't forget we have a wedding to plan, or had you forgotten about that?"

"Hardly, considering we attended a bridal fair this week. I'm still going through the samples I picked up from the other exhibitors."

"Remember what I said: you need to pick up a large sheet of paper—A3 will do—and create a mood board, similar to what interior designers use."

"Yes, Mum. I'll do that at the weekend. Okay, I'd better get on. I hope your day brightens up, Crystal. Thanks for the chat."

"You're welcome anytime. Good luck with what lies ahead of you today."

Sam ended the call and sat back. She stared at her lunch. The hunger pangs that she had felt earlier had now vanished. She closed her eyes, and images of her brother sitting in his cell entered her mind. She felt heartless and guilty at the same time for blocking him out of her life for years. However, some people in this life refuse point blank to be saved. Mike was one of them, which was galling because, before he went off the rails, all three of them had been really close while growing up.

A knock on the door brought her out of her reverie. "Hi, Bob, what's up?"

"I thought I'd check if you were all right." He stepped into the room and closed the door. Flopping into the chair, he pointed at her lunch. "I thought you were hungry."

"I was, but after speaking with Crystal, I've gone off the thought of eating."

He frowned. "May I ask why?"

"She raised a couple of horrors from our past, and it got me thinking, that's all."

"Care to share?"

"Not really. I sent her the photo of the bloke Helen was arguing with, but she couldn't put a name to him or even tell me if he was another exhibitor."

"That's a shame. I suppose the day would have been hectic for Crystal. She probably wouldn't have had time to speak with the other people attending the fair, apart from the customers, that is."

"True."

"What else aren't you telling me? There are deeper lines in your brow, so don't try to pull the wool over my eyes."

She smiled and instinctively rubbed at her forehead.

He snorted. "That won't help."

"I know. I can't remember how the conversation started, but we ended up talking about Mike and Chris."

Bob tilted his head. "Your ex, Chris?"

"Yep, and my brother."

"Blimey, I had forgotten all about your brother. I take it he's still inside, is he?"

"Yes, although I think he's up for parole soon."

"Why did his name crop up? Or am I being too nosey?"

"No, don't be silly. From what I can remember, Crystal asked if I had heard from him."

"And have you?"

"No, not a dickey bird, which suits me."

"Then I'd leave well alone. You wouldn't want to cause trouble for yourself, Sam."

"Meaning?"

"If he's sat there, stewing in a cell all day, and you get in touch with him out of the blue..."

Sam nodded. "I get where you're coming from. For your information, I've got no intention of getting in touch with him. It was just a passing question from my sister."

"That apparently has stirred up a lot of memories for you, judging by your lack of appetite, which is a rarity."

Sam chuckled and reached for her sandwich but didn't get the chance to open it because her phone rang. "This might be Davina calling back." She answered it. "Hello, DI Sam Cobbs speaking. How may I help?"

"Sam, it's Des Markham. I wanted to let you know that the techs found Helen's phone at the house. They're bringing it into the lab as we speak."

"Wow, that's brilliant. Is it locked?"

"That's a daft question," Des replied. "I'm not sure if I know anyone who doesn't lock their phone these days."

"I'll get Bob to call Jason, ask him if he knows the passcode."

Bob stood and gestured to Sam that he would call Jason outside and left the room.

"Can you hold on? Bob has nipped out of the office to call the husband. Or do you want me to ring you back?"

"No, I'm free for the next five minutes or so. We can participate in small talk for a while."

"Oh, right," she stammered, not expecting that answer from him—the pathologist who detested any form of idle chitchat.

He laughed. "That's caught you on the hop, hasn't it?"

Sam chuckled. "You're not wrong. Umm… I don't suppose you've heard from Helen's parents, have you?"

"Not as far as I know. What are their names?"

"Linda and Matthew Baldwin."

"That's a negative. I take it they're keen to see her."

"The mother is. Although I did try to dissuade her, what with her dying in a fire."

"Let's just say I wouldn't want to view a member of my family in the same situation."

"Yeah, but you're wise."

"About as wise as you, Inspector."

"Just a second, Bob's back. Any luck?" she asked her partner, more out of hope than expectation.

Bob screwed up his lips and shook his head. "He doesn't know it."

"Never mind. Sorry, Des, it's a no-go from the husband, which means it is down to your guys to come up trumps for us."

"No change there then," Des quipped. "I'm off. I can't stand any more of this scintillating conversation." He ended the call abruptly before Sam could respond.

"His rudeness never fails to annoy me. Hopefully, the techs will be able to get into her phone soon. In the meantime, we could get on to the provider and obtain a list of recent calls and phone numbers."

"I'll have a word with Claire, see what she can come up with. Now get that sandwich down your neck before I steal it. Do you want a fresh cup of coffee?"

Sam grinned. "You're an angel, thanks, mate." She picked up the sandwich and tore the corner of the packet. By the time Bob had returned, she had devoured half of it.

He placed her mug in front of her and took a step back. "Selfish. I was looking forward to that."

She offered him the other half. "Be my guest. I'm not sure I could eat a whole one."

"If you're sure? You know me, I'm never one for turning down food."

Sam pushed the sandwich towards him. He pounced on it and bit into it as if he hadn't eaten for days.

"You're a pig. I have every sympathy with your wife."

"I'll be sure to let her know when I get home tonight."

"How is Abigail?"

He frowned and finished his mouthful before he replied. "Fine. Why?" he asked suspiciously.

"Why do you always think there's an ulterior motive when I ask about your family?"

"Because you rarely ask after them."

"Touché. I'm asking now."

"And I've already told you, she's fine. Is this about your brother?"

"No, it is not. What makes you think that?"

"Call it a hunch. Okay, what next?"

"Well, you couldn't be further from the truth. Next, while we wait for Davina to get back to us, I think we should take a ride out to Helen's place of work. Maybe one of her colleagues will be able to tell us who the man she was arguing with is."

4

"What kind of name is that?" Bob queried, the closer they got to the trading estate where Spark and Shine Events were based.

"Search me. I suppose it has a certain ring to it." Out of her peripheral vision, she saw his head jerk her way.

"Are you for real? Next road on the right."

"Yes, boss. People try to be fancy with business names these days. I believe this isn't the first time you've raised the subject either."

"Pardon me for breathing. I was trying to make polite conversation, ensuring I steer clear of the topic of our families." He huffed out a breath and folded his arms.

She patted him on the leg. "And you appear to have lost your sense of humour at the same time. Is this it?"

"Yes, this is the place. Not the type of business you'd usually find on a trading estate, is it?"

"Hmm... you read my mind. Maybe most of their business comes from online sources, and they prefer to meet customers elsewhere rather than have them drop by here for a chat."

"You know, you talk a lot of sense, sometimes."

Sam couldn't help it. She let out a full belly laugh. "You crack me up without even trying. Let's see what they have to say. I'll just make sure my phone is switched on, just in case Davina tries to call me."

"Maybe she's busy at work and they don't allow the staff to spend all day on their phones."

They got out of the car, and Sam continued the conversation on their walk. "Is that what you'd do if you ran a business?"

"Too bloody right. I reckon too many businesses go to the wall these days because of the staff taking the piss with their boss."

"Wow, you're really in a grumpy mood today."

"My best friend's wife has been killed. I think I'm entitled to be a bit grouchy."

"Grouchy, yes, but you're going OTT, matey. Let's try to keep a lid on our true feelings during this trip, okay?"

He shrugged. "Suits me. Lead on."

Sam opened the door to the unit. Just inside was a small reception area. A woman in her fifties removed her spectacles and rose from her chair.

"Hello there. I'm Janet. How may I help you?"

Sam and Bob flashed their warrant cards.

"DI Sam Cobbs and DS Bob Jones. Is it possible to speak to whoever is in charge, please?"

"Oh my goodness! Yes, of course. I'll see if Mr Kendrick is free."

"Thank you."

The woman scurried through the door behind her desk. Sam and Bob scanned the articles pinned to the wall.

"This is Helen at another bridal fair by the look of it," Sam said.

"Yes, that's her. She was beautiful, wasn't she?"

Sam picked up on the sadness in her partner's tone. "Are you all right?"

"Yeah, I will be. If I find it hard to cope, I'll make my excuses and wait in the car, if that's okay with you?"

"Of course it is. You can go now if you want. I can handle this by myself, Bob."

"I'll see how I go. I don't want to let you down."

"You could never do that. I understand how difficult this must be for you."

The door opened, and Janet reappeared with a smartly dressed man in his late forties beside her. Janet made the introductions.

"The police? Do you want to come through to my office?"

"Yes, that might be best, sir," Sam agreed.

Kendrick smiled uncomfortably. "Very well. Come this way. Janet, can you arrange for some refreshments to be brought in to us, please?"

"Thank you for the offer, but we'll decline. We've not long had lunch," Sam replied, much to Bob's disgust, who grunted beside her.

Kendrick led the way through the cavernous warehouse to an office at the rear. He removed a couple of chairs from the stack outside the room and placed them in front of his desk. "Please, take a seat. I'm Neil, by the way."

"Have you been here long?" Sam asked.

She and Bob sat.

"Around ten years, give or take a few months. We celebrated our tenth anniversary back in December. The business is going from strength to strength, although there were times, back in 2020, when I thought about throwing in the towel."

"A lot of businesses folded during the pandemic. I'm glad your trade recovered. I was at the bridal fair at Muncaster Castle. The event was second to none."

"Thank you, that was down to our events' manager, Helen. Do you mind telling me what you're doing here?"

"Actually, it's to do with Helen."

His brow furrowed, and he picked up a pen and twisted it through his fingers. "If you're here to speak with her, I'm afraid she's not here today."

"We know."

His frown deepened. "Am I missing something? What do you mean, you know?"

"We were called out to an incident at Helen's home this morning."

He sat upright and placed the pen on his desk. "And? I've been trying to call her every half an hour this morning. It's not like her to ignore my calls. Has something happened to her?"

"Unfortunately, Helen lost her life in a fire at her home."

His hands shook and slapped against his cheeks. "She what? This can't be true... Helen, gone? This can't be happening. She was... so full of life." He shook his head repeatedly, clearly in shock. Then he opened the drawer of his desk, removed a bottle of whisky and a tumbler and poured himself a drink. "Sorry, you don't mind, do you?"

"Go ahead. I appreciate how much of a shock it must be to hear about a colleague's death."

He gulped down a large mouthful of whisky and shook his head. "She was more than that. She was the heart of this company. The key person who brought in about eighty to ninety percent of the business."

"Oh, I see."

He swivelled in his chair to face the wall behind him. Sam and Bob stared at each other and shrugged. Neil remained that way for several more minutes while he finished off his drink, and when he turned back to face them again, Sam studied his features and noticed there were tears in his eyes.

"Are you all right?" she asked.

"Not really. I'm shell-shocked, if you must know. Not since my father passed away has a piece of news impacted me like this. I'm sorry. Please give me a moment, if you wouldn't mind."

He left his chair and raced out of the room.

"Wow, what the fuck was that all about?" Bob peered over his shoulder and said.

"You tell me. A tad over the top, wasn't it?" Sam's curiosity rose the longer Neil was absent from the room.

Eventually, he returned and took his place behind the desk. "Please forgive me. I'm not one for handling news of this magnitude very well."

"It's okay, take your time."

"But why are you here? If it's to break the news, couldn't her husband have called in and told us?"

"As you can imagine, Jason is beside himself. He was away on a course. He drove back this morning, and that's where we met him—at the house."

"I'm glad he showed up. That's not always the case."

Sam sighed. "Can I ask what you mean by that?"

"I shouldn't really be speaking out of turn, but their marriage was in tatters. We were all aware of it around here."

Sam's interest piqued. "She told you that?"

"Yes, everyone knew."

"When you say in tatters, are you suggesting their marriage was on the rocks?"

"I don't know if it had gone that far, but from what I can gather, they didn't tend to spend much time with each other."

Bob withdrew his notebook and jotted down some notes. Sam was relieved he was keeping quiet and not jumping in with two feet to question Neil.

"That's interesting. We'll chase that up when we leave here. Has Helen had any issues with customers lately?"

He shook his head and topped up his glass with more of the malt whisky. "No. She was an utter professional. She was adept at putting the customers' needs first. I don't understand why you're asking these questions when I've already told you that her marriage was in the toilet," he replied, a note of bitterness evident in his tone.

"Because her husband was away on business when the fire started," Bob chipped in, sticking up for his friend.

"What does that matter? People can be bought. What's to say he didn't pay someone to kill his wife, knowing that he had a solid alibi? Isn't that what criminals do?"

Sam paused to contemplate his suggestion for a moment, then asked, "Do you know Jason well?"

"We've met up occasionally. I wouldn't say I've got a lot in common with the man. It's not obligatory to get on with your employees' spouses."

"You seem offended by the question, Neil. Can you explain why?"

"You're guilty of misinterpreting what I'm telling you. That's not my problem."

"We're leading a murder investigation."

"Well, don't look at me; I didn't start the fire."

"I didn't say you did. Why don't you tell us about Helen and her role in the company?" Sam smiled, trying to calm him down and get him back onside.

"She was the events' manager. She has three members of staff on her team."

It was then that Sam remembered the photo. She pulled out her phone and scrolled through to locate it. "Is this man familiar to you?"

Neil took the phone from her for a closer look and then shook his head. "No. Who is he?"

"Someone of interest. The cameras at the castle captured him having a dispute with Helen."

"Is that so? She didn't tell me that someone had confronted her, neither did the rest of the staff who attended the event with Helen."

"Perhaps they didn't know," Sam replied. "Would it be possible to speak with them? Are they here?"

"They are. They're getting everything ready for another event, which is taking place in Whitehaven tomorrow. That's why I've been trying to call Helen all morning. It would have been her job to organise the team."

"I know how busy they're likely to be, but would it be all right if we had a brief chat with them?" she repeated, sensing that he'd dodged her original question.

"Yes, feel free. However, please bear in mind that they need to get everything arranged by the end of the day."

"We'll be as quick as possible, I promise."

"Will you give me five minutes, so I can tell the team about Helen?"

"Of course."

He left the room.

As soon as the door closed behind him, Bob leaned over and whispered, "I don't like him."

Sam sniggered. "Why? Because he pointed a finger at Jason?"

"Not really. He's just coming across, I don't know... kind of weird. Who the fuck brings out a bottle of malt when being interviewed by the cops?"

"Neil Kendrick, that's who. You heard him. He told us that Helen brought in between eighty to ninety percent of their revenue. Sounds to me like he's already counting the cost of losing her."

"If she had an important job here, then that would go without saying, surely. A bit like if something happened to you... the rest of the team would be lost. Unable to function properly."

Sam tutted and slapped his arm. "Hush now. I'm being serious."

"Yeah, so was I."

The door opened, and Neil marched back into the room. "They can spare you thirty minutes. They're due to pack up the vehicles and head over to the location to start setting up the venue."

Sam shot out of the chair. "That's fine by us. Can you take us to them?"

"I have calls to make. I hope you don't mind. I've arranged for Janet to take you."

"Excellent, thanks. I'll give you one of my cards. If anything should come to mind when we leave, feel free to give me a call."

"Thanks, I'll keep it handy. I hope you find the person who took Helen away from us."

"We won't stop searching for the person responsible for her death. Thank you for seeing us today."

"Hopefully, the staff will be able to fill in some blanks for you. They're the ones who worked alongside her most days."

"Let's hope so."

Sam and Bob exited the room, and Janet showed them through the cavernous warehouse to a smaller room at the back. Two men and a woman stopped filling the boxes near the racking and approached them. Janet made the introductions again.

"I'll be at my desk if you need me."

Sam thanked her and then spoke to the woman, "Cathy, was it?"

"Yes, that's right. We were shocked to learn that Helen had lost her life. What can we do to help you?"

Sam removed her phone from her pocket and showed the three colleagues the photo of the man at the castle. "Do any of you know him?"

"Hmm... I recognise him," Cathy announced. "I was at the castle with Helen yesterday. Who is he?"

"We're interested in speaking with him. We have obtained footage of Helen and this man arguing in the castle hallway."

"Oh no. I think he was lending a hand to one of the exhibitors. Now, who was it? Excuse me while I get the file for the tables at the castle." She went through a doorway off to the right that Sam hadn't noticed. She returned with a coloured plastic wallet. She flicked through the papers and removed a plan. "I can get you a copy of this. It shows all the exhibitors."

"How wonderful! That would be a great help. Thank you."

Cathy raced back into the room and swiftly joined them again with the extra sheet, which she handed to Sam. "I've had a quick look, and I think I saw him hanging around with this woman here. Theresa makes exceptional wedding cakes. I think I have her card here." She searched through the file again and withdrew a business card.

Sam took it and angled it so Bob could write the number in his notebook. "That's amazing, thanks. Did you notice anything amiss at the castle yesterday?"

"Nothing really. Oh yes, the staff at the castle had to deal with a small fire, but it was put out swiftly. Apart from that, Helen and I were flying around most of the day. We always are at such events. It's important for bridal fairs to be a success. Our clients pay a lot and pull out all the stops to ensure everything goes well on the day. First impressions count when customers have a large budget to spend on their big day."

"Of course it does. I was at the bridal fair myself as a customer. Crystal, who owns the bridal boutique in Workington, is my sister. I was there when news spread about the fire. It was something and nothing."

"I thought I recognised you. We passed each other briefly a couple of times during the day. Crystal has fabulous gowns. I'm getting married next year. My boyfriend doesn't know it yet, though." She laughed. "I intend to buy my dress from Crystal. We've already had a quick chat about the design. She's keeping her eye open for me."

Her two male colleagues pulled faces behind her back.

She sensed them taking the mickey out of her and spun around. "Pack it in. You're only jealous."

"Of what? Ralf hasn't even mentioned getting married. It's all in your head, Cathy," the man wearing a suit teased.

"Shut up, Warren. We've discussed it a few times, not that it's any of your business. There's no chance of you getting married anytime soon because no one will have you."

The other man and Cathy both laughed, but Warren snarled and said something indecipherable, then marched towards the van and started loading the vehicle.

"Ouch. That's put him in a bad mood for the rest of the day," Cathy said.

"Lack of a sense of humour will get you nowhere, especially these days," the other man said.

"Sorry, I didn't catch your name," Sam asked him.

"I'm Eric, and he's our boss, Warren. He was Helen's second-in-command. He's wound up about what happened to Helen. He'll calm down soon." He peered over his shoulder and then leaned in and said, "He'd better. It'll be a long afternoon if his foul mood continues."

"Yeah, I hadn't considered that," Cathy agreed. "We were all shocked to hear about Helen. We all thought the world of her. She wasn't like a normal boss. She treated us all like friends as well as colleagues. Valued our input during meetings, that sort of thing. Luckily, we're all on the same wavelength around here."

"She did," Eric added. "It won't be the same without her."

Sam's phone rang. She glanced at the caller ID to see Des' name lit up. "If you'll excuse me. I have to take this." She stepped away a few feet and answered the call. "Hi, Des. Sorry for the delay. What can I do for you?"

"It's more about what I can do for you, Sam."

His voice sounded upbeat for a change, which raised her spirits. "Have you got some news for me?"

"I have. We've gained access to Helen's phone."

"That's great news. And?"

"And around the time of her death, she received a text message from a bloke called Warren."

Her gaze shot through the warehouse to the man loading the boxes in the back of the van. "Interesting. I'm here at her place of work now, and about fifty feet away from me is a man called Warren. Can you tell me what the message says?"

"*Missed you today. Still thinking about last night.* Plus, there's this one: *can't wait to see you again...*"

"Hmm... the plot thickens. Thanks, Des. I don't suppose you can check his number in the contacts for me?"

"Already done. I'll text it to you now."

"You're a gem. It'll be hard for him to deny the message was from him if I can prove it."

"Exactly. I hope it works a charm for you. If anything else comes to light, I'll let you know. Are you going to collect the phone?"

"Yes, we'll drop by on our way back to the station. Thanks again, great teamwork."

"If you say so." He ended the call.

Sam waited a few seconds and then opened her phone again when the text came through. She returned to the group and excused Bob so that she could fill him in.

"What's going on?" he asked.

Sam told him the news and said, "I think we need to have a chat with Warren, on his own."

"What if it's not him?"

"Des has sent me the phone number from which the text message was sent. If he tries to deny it, I'll give that a call."

"Crafty mare."

She winked at him. "How have you got on with the others?"

"They knew her marriage was dodgy but none of them could tell me if she'd fallen out with anyone lately."

"Okay. Let's dismiss them and concentrate all our efforts on Warren for now."

"I agree."

They returned to where Cathy and Eric were waiting for them. "Thanks for all your help. We've had an urgent call for us to attend an incident. I'll give you both one of my cards. If anything should come to mind regarding Helen, feel free to give me a call."

They both accepted the card and then went back to packing the boxes. Sam and Bob walked towards the back of the van.

Warren glanced up and eyed them warily. He paused and dropped the box he was holding. "Is something wrong?"

"You tell us," Sam shot back at him.

He crossed his arms and tapped his foot. "I'm a very busy man, Inspector, with a deadline to keep."

"I'm aware. Why did you send Helen a message the night of her death?"

His arms dropped, and the colour rose in his cheeks. "I... umm... I didn't."

Sam said nothing further. Instead, she punched in the number Des had given her. Seconds later, Warren's phone rang in his pocket. Sam tilted her head. "Don't mind us, answer it."

"No, it can wait. All right, you've got me. Yes, I sent Helen a message the night of the fire."

"And what did it say?"

"I can't remember."

"Let me remind you." She glanced down at her phone to ensure she said the words correct. "*Missed you today. Still thinking about last night*. And the other message, saying, *Can't wait to see you again*... How did I do?"

He closed his eyes and shook his head. "You've got me by the short and curlies. But I didn't hurt her. She didn't reply to my messages. I knew Jason was away for the week. I presumed he had come home early. She didn't usually ignore my messages."

"Were you having an affair?"

"Ssh... please, keep your voice down. No one around here knew."

"Do you want to hold this conversation elsewhere? In an office, perhaps?"

"Yes, I'd prefer that, thank you. Come this way." He led them past a puzzled Cathy and Eric and said, "Continue loading the van; I won't be too long."

"Will do, boss," Eric replied.

Warren showed them into a small room full of filing cabinets. There was a desk shoved in the corner and a few old chairs that had seen better days. "You can risk sitting if you want."

"We'll pass. Thanks all the same," Sam said.

Bob had his pad and pen poised, ready to take down what Warren had to say.

"Why don't you tell us what was going on between you and Helen?"

He closed his eyes and sighed. "I've had to hold it together all morning. I've rung her dozens of times. I knew there was something wrong. I should have been there with her. I might have been able to save her."

"When did you last speak to Helen?"

"Yesterday, she rang me on her way home. I was on the other line with a prospective customer. I couldn't take the call but rang her back as soon as I'd finished. She was driving. She told me she'd ring me later, after she'd eaten. Helen was exhausted after the event she'd organised. I've been worried about her." He swept a hand through his short hair and sniffled. "I can't believe I will never see her again."

"About your affair, how long had it been going on?" Sam asked.

"A while."

"Can you be more specific?"

"A few months. She needed a shoulder to cry on. I was available and lent her mine."

"And one thing led to another and you ended up in bed together, is that it?"

"You make it sound so sordid. It wasn't like that at all. I had true feelings for her."

Sam cocked an eyebrow. "Were they reciprocated?"

"Yes."

"Was she about to leave Jason for you?"

"No, it hadn't gone that far, although I gave her the option of moving in with me."

"Why didn't she? We've heard from several sources that her marriage was in tatters. Were you the cause of that?"

"Hardly. He was having an affair, too."

Sam's head snapped around to see Bob's reaction. He was seething. Sam sensed the steam coming out of his nostrils and ears. She nudged him with her elbow, warning him to keep quiet.

"Who with? What do you know about the affair?"

"That it had been going on for over six months. Helen was devastated. She regarded Jason as the love of her life."

"Did she challenge him about it?"

"I'm not sure. She told me she found something in the footwell of Jason's car. I believe it was a small pouch with some makeup in it. When she tackled him about it, he tried to make out that it was hers and that she was losing her mind."

"That's disgusting. Of course she wasn't. Who was the woman?"

"I believe she's someone he met up with on one of these courses he often attends."

Sam nodded. "Her name?"

"Let me think... it's Vanessa something." He paused to think and then clicked his fingers. "Vanessa Mitchell. Yes, that's it."

"Had Helen ever confronted the woman?"

"No. She wasn't the type. I think she was resigned to Jason leaving her for this woman. But Helen was determined that she wasn't going to be the one to leave the house. She adored that cottage. Her parents had a similar one when she was growing up, so it brought back wonderful memories for her."

"I take it she confided in you?"

He nodded.

"Was there anything else upsetting her? Had someone threatened her, perhaps?"

His eyes narrowed, and he shook his head. "No, not that she mentioned. She was devoted to this place. All her spare time was spent creating new events that customers would be interested in at certain times of the year. You know the type of thing—Halloween being a prime example—and, of course, at this time of year, bridal fairs. We have two more to hold over the next two weeks. I'm going to need to step up to the plate and organise those myself. Thankfully, I'll have Cathy and Eric working alongside me. It won't be the same without Helen here, though. She was the heart and soul of this place, something that is just dawning on Neil, I assume. He was having a fit earlier when he couldn't get hold of Helen."

"What does he do around here? If that's not a silly question."

"It's not. I wish I knew. He sits behind that desk of his all day. He tries to tell us that he's drumming up extra business by being on the phone all day long. That's crap. All our business comes from clients with whom we've dealt in the past. So we must be doing something right, eh?"

"That's true. I attended the bridal fair at the castle and was blown away by how organised it was."

"That was down to Helen. She had a magic touch and was always keen on making people's days."

"Did you know?"

He tilted his head. "Know what?"

"That Helen was pregnant?"

He covered his eyes with his hand and turned his back on them. His shoulders rose and fell, and he let out a sob. "I didn't know. I've always wanted kids. I loved her, truly loved her."

"We don't know who the father was. We could ask the pathologist to do a DNA test if you want?"

He faced her once more, an urgency smouldering in his eyes. "Would you? It's something I need to know."

"Okay, I'll have a word with him. Are you going to be all right?"

"Yes, I think so."

"We're going to leave it there for now. I'll give you one of my cards. Have a think later when you have more time on your hands. Let me know if anything comes to mind that Helen might have confided in you over the last few months."

"I'll do that. Good luck with your investigation. I'd be keeping a watchful eye on Jason if I were you. A bit too convenient for him to be away when the house goes up in flames, eh?"

"Don't worry. He's still a suspect in our eyes."

They exited the room, and Warren showed them back to the reception area. Sam could tell Bob was biting his tongue. She shook Warren's hand. He opened the door, and they left the building.

"Don't say a word until we're back in the car," she warned her partner.

She pointed the fob at the car, and the doors clunked open. Sam shot around the driver's side and slipped in behind the steering wheel. "Now it's safe for you to let rip."

"What the fuck? Should we believe him? About Jason?"

"It would make sense. Maybe your best mate is guilty of keeping other things hidden from us."

"I doubt it. I'm as livid as you are about this. Do you want me to give him a call?"

"No, not yet. Let's see if he comes forward with the information first. In the meantime, we should try to find this other woman, Vanessa Mitchell."

"Yeah, I agree. I'll ring Claire, get her working on it now."

"I'm going to stop off at the lab to pick up Helen's phone. By the time we get back, we should have Helen's phone information. You can chase that with Claire while you're speaking with her."

"Will do."

She touched his arm. "Are you all right?"

"I will be, once the truth comes out. It's getting more and more twisted by the hour. My head is spinning."

"Yep, mine is too."

Sam picked up the phone, and they returned to base. Bob remained quiet during the journey. She recognised the signs that he was pissed off. She made them both a coffee and insisted they drink them in her office.

"I have a sinking feeling that a lecture is coming my way," he said, throwing himself into the chair opposite her.

"Not at all. Please take it as a friend looking out for you. We need to consider all the facts. We can't ignore them, Bob. In fact, we'd be downright foolish if we did," Sam said, finally taking her seat. She leaned back and ran her finger around the rim of her mug as she spoke. "Helen and Jason's marriage was on the rocks. We also know they were both having affairs, and we're aware that someone went out of their way to kill her. I know you're going to hate me for proposing this, but I think it's imperative that we start looking closer at Jason, Bob. The fact that he was away doesn't necessarily clear him. What if, as already suggested by Helen's boss, he arranged, or should I say, *paid* someone to burn the house down?"

"I know him. He wouldn't do that."

Sam sighed and moved her head from side to side to ease the tension in her neck.

Bob's eyes flashed with frustration, and his grip tightened on his mug. "You can't seriously think Jason is capable of this. The team has made the necessary searches through his and Helen's bank accounts. If he'd paid someone to start the fire, it would show up on his accounts, wouldn't it?"

Sam tutted. "Ever heard of a cash transaction?"

"Don't treat me like an idiot, Sam, please. Even if he paid cash, he would still have had to withdraw the money from the account."

"Don't get snarky with me. Not necessarily. He might have been putting money aside, under his mattress, for all we know."

Bob shook his head and chewed the inside of his mouth.

Sam took a sip from her mug, giving them both a chance to calm down. "Maybe it wasn't Jason behind her death at all. Perhaps someone else intentionally waited for him to be out of town before they struck. The fact is, someone killed her. She was bludgeoned to death."

"I know she was. I think that's a more likely scenario than Jason paying someone to kill her."

Sam wagged her finger. "Sorry if I misled you. I'm not saying that I have the intention of parking the Jason-paying-someone theory to one side, not yet. I'm just sitting here, with my partner, bouncing ideas around."

He stared at her, his loyalty to Jason clashing with the mounting evidence. "This isn't right, Sam. I can't emphasise it enough. Jason's a good guy. There's no way he'd do something like this."

"I hope you're right," Sam said softly, though her gut told her that there was more to Jason than Bob realised.

"What about the fella in the footage? You seem to have forgotten all about him. There's also the mysterious person on the corner who was spotted before the fire started. Plus, there's Warren. He's just admitted to us that he was having an affair with Helen."

"I'm aware of that, Bob." Sam removed a business card from her pocket. "I'm going to give Theresa a call. See if she can tell us who this man is."

He stood and walked towards the door. "I'll leave you to it. I hope we don't end up falling out over this case, Sam."

"Not in a month of Sundays. Trust the process, Bob. Chase up the patrols who are canvassing the area for me. See if any of the neighbours have cameras at their properties. I have a few calls I need to make."

He grunted and left the room.

Sam rolled her eyes, drank the rest of her coffee and picked up her phone. First, she rang Davina, Helen's sister. The phone rang and rang until the voicemail message kicked in. Sam left her second message of the day on the woman's phone, urging Davina to get back to her ASAP. She hung up feeling dejected. Her phone rang before she could make her second call. She crossed her fingers, hoping it was Davina returning her call. It wasn't.

"Hi, Rhys. How are you?"

"Worried about you. I thought we agreed that you would ring me at lunchtime." He sounded anxious.

She kicked herself for slipping up. "I'm so sorry, I know I promised, but... a new murder investigation came our way this morning, and I haven't stopped all day."

"Okay. I understand. I was worried about you, that's all."

"There's no need. I'm surrounded by a great team. They wouldn't let anything happen to me. How has your day been?"

"Hit and miss. A few of my clients have been no-shows, which always frustrates the hell out of me."

"Bugger. You need to start charging people if they don't cancel at least twenty-four hours before their appointment is due. Other people do."

He sighed. "I know. I need to get my arse into gear where that is concerned."

"Chin up. Do you want me to stop off and pick up something nice for dinner tonight?"

"I was about to ask the same. I'll do it. It sounds like you have enough on your plate as it is."

"You're not wrong. I've still got a few calls to make."

"In other words, piss off and let me get back to work."

Sam gasped. "I would never be that rude."

"I believe you. I'll see you later. I love you. Stay safe."

"Ditto."

She ended the call, desperate to feel his arms around her. She shook off the sensation and focussed on her job, eager to get a few loose ends tied up by the end of the day. She rang Margaret, the Flintoffs' neighbour. With the confirmation of arson, Sam needed more details about that mysterious person spotted near the house on the night of the fire. Who were they, and what was their connection to Helen?

"Hello. Who is this?" Margaret asked suspiciously.

"Hello, Margaret. There's no need for you to be concerned. This is DI Sam Cobbs. We met earlier. I'm the Senior Investigating Officer in charge of the Flintoff case."

"Oh, yes, I remember. How is the investigation going? Is there any news about the fire?" The woman sounded relieved to be speaking with Sam.

"I'm sorry to have to inform you that we believe the fire was started deliberately. Which means we're treating this as a murder investigation now."

"What? I don't believe it. Murder? Oh my God…"

"Are you up to answering some more questions?"

"I'm not sure what else I can tell you. I've been sitting here thinking about the situation, but nothing has come to mind. I want to help, I really do. I liked Helen. I didn't know her that well… Sorry, I'm going on and not letting you get a word in edgeways."

"It's okay. Feel free to chat. No pressure from me. I know how upsetting this must be for you."

"I've been a nervous wreck all day, thankful that my house is detached. Otherwise, I might have been killed in my bed if the fire had spread out of control."

"I agree. You were very fortunate. You mentioned hearing arguments between Helen and Jason, and you also saw someone at the end of the road. Can you tell me if you saw or heard anything else unusual in the days leading up to the fire?"

Margaret fell quiet for a moment. "I've been thinking about nothing else since you left. I racked my brain and realised that I had seen that person several times in the past week or so. I appeared at my window one day, and they dipped their head and ran off when they saw me looking at them. I know you're going to ask me for a better description of them, but I won't be able to give you one because they always wore a hoodie. They never came that close to the house for me to get a better look at them."

"Were they specifically watching the Flintoffs' house?"

"I couldn't swear in a court of law that was the case, so you'll have to forgive me. I didn't think much of it at the time, but now... it does seem suspicious, doesn't it?"

"Was there anything that stood out about them? Could you tell how tall they were?"

"No, it's hard to say when I only caught a glimpse of them from a distance. I couldn't even tell you what age they were or what colour hair they had, or whether it was long or short. I'm so sorry. I feel as though I'm letting you down."

"Nonsense, please, you've been brilliant. I'll let you go. Please, try not to let this consume you."

"I'll try. If I think of anything else, I'll let you know."

"I can't ask for more than that. Take care, and thank you for speaking with me, Margaret."

"Good luck. I really mean that. The thought of Helen dying at the hands of someone else is very disturbing. I rang my son; he asked me to stay with him for a few days. I was reluctant at first, but he insisted and is picking me up after he finishes work."

"That's a wise decision. I'd feel better if you stayed elsewhere for a few days, too." Sam hung up and returned to the incident room. Her head throbbing, she walked over to her partner's desk. "How are you?"

"Fine. You?" he replied abruptly.

"I tried calling Davina again. No luck. Then I contacted Jason's neighbour. She revealed a bit more about this strange person hanging around."

That snippet of information caught his attention, and he glanced up at her. "Wow. Why the heck didn't she tell us that earlier?"

"She admitted that the devastation of waking up to the fire had knocked her for six. She's worried about staying at her house tonight, so she's going to stay with her son for the time being. She's old, Bob. We have to make exceptions for the elderly in our society now and then."

He leaned his head back and tutted. "I guess. Where do we go from here?"

"Whoever this mystery person is, they were watching the house. I think it's time we start delving deeper into Helen's family and friends. There's something we're missing." Sam peered over her shoulder at Claire and asked, "Any luck obtaining the phone records?" When they had arrived back at the station, Sam had handed Helen's phone to Claire to go through.

"I've compared them to the calls that she had received over the past week. They matched perfectly, except this one number. She deleted it from her recent calls list."

Claire showed her the number.

"Do we know who it belongs to?"

"I haven't had a chance to research that yet, boss."

Sam removed her phone from her pocket and rang the number.

"Hello, Vanessa speaking."

Sam's eyes widened, and she promptly ended the call.

"Well? Don't keep us in suspense. Who was it?" Bob bounced out of his chair and asked.

"Vanessa. I'm assuming it was Vanessa Mitchell. The person Jason is having an affair with."

"What the fu...?" Bob said. "Why would she ring Helen?"

"Are you kidding me? I doubt if it was to exchange Christmas cake recipes."

"Don't be sarcastic. I'm serious. If Abigail was having an affair, I wouldn't ring her lover. I might go round there and throttle the bastard."

Sam chuckled. "You do surprise me. I'm inclined to agree with you. I wouldn't ring someone if Rhys was doing the dirty on me with them." She thought back to when Chris, her former husband, had cheated on her and she had challenged his lover in person, who also happened to be a solicitor who had represented a criminal at the station.

"We need to speak with her."

Bob looked at the clock on the wall. It was getting on for six. "What, now?"

"No. First thing in the morning. I need a clear head to tackle her."

Her phone buzzed. She removed her phone from her pocket once more and read the message that had arrived. It was from the forensic team.

An initial report was back about the fire. Sam's heart raced as she opened it.

Fingerprints had been found on a small, scorched container near the fireplace—the container used to pour the petrol.

One set of prints matched Helen's, but there was another set.

"What's that?" Bob asked.

She gave him the phone and relayed the information to the rest of the team. "A second set of fingerprints have been found on a container at the house."

"Okay, we'd better start collecting fingerprints then," Bob suggested.

"You know as well as I do that we're not supposed to do that unless the person is a suspect."

"Bugger. I hate that rule."

"You're not the only one. Okay, folks. Let's call it a day."

During the drive home, Sam contemplated how far they had got with the investigation. On the one hand, she was pleased by how much ground they had covered and how many people she and Bob had interviewed. However, on the other, she felt gutted not to have spoken with Davina, despite her best efforts to contact Helen's sister.

She continued the journey on autopilot and drew up outside her cottage ten minutes later. Rhys was already home. She assumed he would have collected Sonny from her neighbour, Doreen, and taken him for a walk, along with his own dog, Casper, who usually went to the office with him.

Doreen appeared at her lounge window, waved and blew Sam a kiss. Sam waved back and raised her thumb, asking if her elderly neighbour was okay. Doreen smiled and nodded, then returned to her seat, presumably to watch TV for the rest of the evening. In a way, Sam envied her, aware of the hours of note-making that lay ahead of her, once dinner was out of the way.

She opened the door, and within seconds, both dogs had appeared, requiring their usual amount of fuss before she had a chance to remove her coat and shoes. "Hey, pups. How are you? Have you been good?"

Sonny and Casper barked and turned in circles, excited to see her. She ruffled their heads and kissed the tips of their noses. Rhys' laughter startled her. "Oops, caught in the act again."

He came to greet her with open arms. She walked into them and linked hers around his waist.

"Something smells good."

"I take it you're referring to the dinner?"

"Let me think about that for a moment or two." She sniffed his neck and kissed it. "Yes, I can confirm, it's the dinner."

He chuckled and patted her on the backside. "It's nearly ready if you want to get changed."

"What would I do without you?"

"Probably starve. I think you'd cope in the main, though, don't you?"

"No way. Not in a million years." The recent attack on him had proved how much he meant to her.

"Hey, stop that," he warned. He placed a finger under her chin, forcing her to look at him.

"Sorry. I can't help it. I think about how close I got to losing you, and it overwhelms me at times."

"There's no need. I'm here with you, and that won't change, not if I can help it. Mind you, if I piss you off, feel free to kick me and Casper out, won't you?"

She stared at him, her mouth gaping open for a moment. She recovered to tell him, "Hey, that was uncalled for. I'd never kick you out. I love having Casper around."

It was his turn to gape at her, then they both ended up laughing.

"You worried me there, for a moment."

She kissed him and ran up the stairs. "Nothing like keeping your man on his toes. I won't be long." She removed her clothes on the way to the bedroom and placed them on the chair by the wardrobe. The need to have a shower was too much to resist. She ran the water, dived under the spray and was in and out within a few minutes. Feeling refreshed, she pulled a comb through her hair, slipped into her leisure suit and returned downstairs to find Rhys serving up their meal, the two dogs sitting by his side.

"I've told you to get in your baskets. I'll save you some and you can have it after we've eaten, you cheeky sods. Now, shoo!"

"Allow me." Sam clicked her fingers. "Sonny, Casper, in your baskets. Now."

Both dogs scampered across the kitchen and bowed their heads in shame.

"Ooo... you can be so masterful," Rhys quipped.

She walked up behind him and hooked her arms around his waist. "Don't you know it?" Releasing her grip, she asked, "What can I do to help?"

"Get the cutlery out."

Sam stole a chip from one of the plates and laid the table. "Fancy a glass of wine?"

"Why not? There's still half a bottle in the fridge. I bought an extra one at the supermarket as well."

"Thanks for thinking of me."

"Of us. I enjoy a glass with my dinner as well. Are you hungry?"

"Always."

She sat at the table, poured the wine and snuck a glance at the dogs, who had both settled down in their respective beds.

"I'm such a cruel dad." He placed the plates, with ample amounts of steak, chips, mushrooms, tomatoes and mangetout on the table.

"You are. They'll be fine. I'll save them some of my steak."

"You will not. I bought an extra one as a treat for them."

Sam's eyes widened. "Blimey, that must have cost you."

"They're worth it." He raised his glass and chinked it against hers. "To us. Bon appetite."

"Ditto. It smells delicious. I'm ready for this after the day I've had."

"Do you want to talk about it? Without going over the gruesome details, of course."

"No, I'd rather chill out and enjoy my meal. Thank you for looking after me so well."

"My pleasure. Are we going to have enough time to go over the plans for the wedding? Or would you rather put that on hold until the weekend?"

"At the weekend would be preferable, if that's all right with you?"

"Suits me."

AFTER THEIR MEAL, Rhys volunteered to feed the dogs and clear up the kitchen, allowing Sam to make some notes about what she wanted to ask Vanessa in the morning. He joined her with a second glass of wine for them both.

She leaned over and kissed him. "Thanks for this evening."

"It's been my pleasure. I like to take my role of caring for you seriously."

"You don't have to. We're equal partners in this relationship."

"I know we are, but I won't stop trying to spoil you, if or when the opportunity arises. You impress me day in and day out, pounding the streets, hunting down criminals, when all I do is sit in an office, listening to my clients sound off about how dire their lives are and how badly their families treat them."

"Hey, that's an extremely tough job. I know I couldn't do it. Maybe occasionally, but not every day of the week. You're a saint."

"So, do you want to tell me about your day? You told me earlier that you're dealing with a murder investigation. Do you have any leads? Any evidence or clues at this point about who the murderer is?"

She took a sip of wine. "I wish. We've been from one side of Workington to the other today, questioning the victim's family and work colleagues. Did I mention that Bob knows the family?"

"No, when we spoke earlier, you didn't give me any of the details."

She sighed, and a sadness swept over her as she filled him in. "I had to call Crystal to share the news. She knew Helen quite well, through work. I met her a couple of times throughout the day at the castle. She was very attentive, keen to help the exhibitors with any issues they might have during the event. Hard to imagine someone like that being killed."

"How did the husband take it?"

"As expected. As the day progressed, it came to light that they were both having affairs."

Rhys sat upright and stared at her. "What? Bloody hell, what is wrong with people? Wouldn't that put the husband as your number one suspect?"

"It should do. I've been battling wills with Bob all day. He's adamant that Jason wouldn't have it in him to kill his wife."

"How well does Bob really know the couple, though?"

"That's the question. I'm not sure he knows them that well, although he insists Jason is one of his best friends. I think it's a case of people seeing less of each other once married life kicks in."

"I can understand that. But if Bob reckons his friend isn't capable of ending his wife's life, then who could the murderer be?"

"Several other clues have come to our attention during the day. We obtained footage from the cameras at the castle. It showed Helen arguing with a man. We know his name. We need to drop round and see him in the morning, as well as with Vanessa, the husband's bit on the side."

"Oh yeah, she would have to be a suspect as well, wouldn't she?"

"Yep. Something else came to our attention just before we left work: the lover has been calling Helen."

"What? How do you know?"

"We obtained Helen's phone records. The lab managed to unlock her phone earlier this afternoon, which led us to her lover, Warren, who we tackled at her workplace. He was her colleague."

"God, you have been busy. Well done for piecing all of this together so quickly."

Sam raised a hand. "I'm guessing that we've only just scratched the surface and there's a lot more to come."

"I don't know how you do it, Sam. I wouldn't know where to start." He chinked his glass against hers. "To my amazing fiancée, who always gets her man, or woman."

She laughed. "Not every time, but most of the time. I have to admit, there are some cases that absolutely do my head in during an investigation."

"Yeah, but you always seem to successfully overcome the obstacles you encounter. Take your last investigation, involving me."

"As if I needed reminding. I had a desire to get that one solved ASAP."

"I know you did, but it still perplexes me to this day how you tracked the bastards down."

"Teamwork. I'm surrounded by the best the Force has to offer."

"Let's hope they don't let you down this time."

"They won't. I have every confidence in them."

"And Bob?"

"He might be wavering at the moment, but I'm sure he'll come good in the end. Right, I'm going to have to continue to make some notes for tomorrow now, that is, if you don't mind?"

"Go for it. There's a documentary on the box that I missed at the weekend which caught my eye."

"Oh, what's it about?"

"Henry the Eighth."

Sam smiled and kissed him. "Enjoy, let me know if it's interesting and I'll watch it at the weekend."

"Okay. Good luck with your notes. Don't work too hard, though. You still need your rest, Sam."

"I know. Thanks for understanding." She took her glass with her and sat at the kitchen table, even though she was tempted to go to bed, which was what she would have done had she been single. First, she tried to call Davina. Again, the woman didn't answer, which concerned her. She added popping around to visit Davina to the top of her to-do list for the morning.

. . .

Rhys checked in on her an hour later and caught her resting her eyes. "Come on, Sam, call it a day, sweetheart."

"Sorry. Yes, I've had it for the day. How was the programme?"

"Very interesting. I think you'd like it. I've paused it so we can watch it together over the weekend. Shall we go to bed?"

Sam yawned and stretched her arms over her head. "I think so. I'll see to the dogs first."

"No, I'll do it. You go up."

"If you're sure?"

Sonny and Casper both sat beside her, vying for attention. She ruffled their heads and sent them out into the garden, once they had returned, she picked up her notebook and headed for the stairs.

Her legs felt like they belonged to someone else, but eventually, she made it to the top. After brushing her teeth, she collapsed into bed and didn't wake until the alarm went off at seven.

5

Bob pulled into the car park ahead of her. He acknowledged her in his rearview mirror. After parking in their respective spaces, they met up at the main entrance.

"How are you this morning, Bob?"

"Truthfully?"

"Of course."

"I barely slept a wink. I rang Jason last night to check how he was."

"And?"

"He broke down. I've never known him to do that before, Sam. There's no way he killed Helen. Whether he was having an affair or not. He swore blind that he loved her."

Sam groaned. "Seriously? You can't still love someone and do the dirty on them at the same time."

"Says you." He turned his back on her and entered the building.

She caught up with him at the security door. "Yes, says me. The voice of experience talking. Chris still professed to love me, despite cheating on me. He was a born liar."

"Oh God, here we go."

Frustrated, she jabbed him in the back as he opened the door, and they walked through it.

"Hey, I can have you for abuse," he said.

"Bollocks, you wouldn't dare."

He smiled, easing the tension between them. "Just kidding. Seriously, though, Jason was beside himself last night. I was tempted to meet up with him, to offer him a shoulder to cry on, but Abigail warned me not to get too involved."

They climbed the stairs.

"I agree with Abigail, especially in the circumstances."

He faced her and frowned. "You still have him at the top of your list of suspects, don't you?"

"Sorry, but yes, until we have enough proof otherwise to dismiss him."

"What you're effectively telling me is that what I believe doesn't matter."

Sam stopped and wagged her finger. "That's bullshit and you know it."

"Is it? I've known him for most of my life. I trust him, Sam. I don't know what else I can say to convince you of his innocence."

"Then stop trying because all it is doing is causing conflict between us."

He grunted and marched ahead of her, then he threw something over his shoulder at her. "You'd be the same if one of your mates was under the microscope."

"You're probably right. Bob, I don't want to fall out about this. We've got a hectic day ahead of us. Can we please agree to differ on this and reassess at the end of each working day?"

"Whatever. In my opinion, he's innocent. All right, look at it this way," he said as he reached the landing and faced her. "If he wanted to kill her, would he seriously take his home and all his possessions out in the process?"

Sam shrugged. He had a point, but then, if he intended to move in with Vanessa, the insurance money would come in handy, except, many companies didn't pay out if arson was involved. "All right, I hear you. Let's see what the day brings and discuss it later."

"Where are we going first today?"

"I think it's important for us to question this mystery man first. When I spoke to Theresa, she confirmed he's called Brian Hanson. Then we can visit Vanessa afterwards."

"What about the sister, Davina?"

"We can slot in a visit to her as well. I tried calling her again last night at around nine. She still didn't answer."

"What do you make of that?"

"I'm not sure what to make of it. Maybe she's rejecting my number after speaking with her parents. Perhaps she's too upset to talk to me. Or she might be out of town. Or maybe the murderer has tracked her down… Oh God, I should have thought about that scenario earlier. We need to visit her first thing—like now." Sam ran back down the stairs with a complaining Bob close behind her.

"Wait! Are you sure about this, Sam?"

"Yes, my gut is telling me something is wrong."

"And yet your gut didn't give you an inkling about her yesterday. How come?"

They tore through the reception area and brushed past Oliver and Liam, who held the door open for them.

"What's wrong, boss?" Oliver asked.

"Bob will give you a call to fill you in. We have to go."

"I will?" Bob asked.

"Get in the car and stop questioning everything I bloody say. It's getting tedious."

He pulled a face at her and jumped into the passenger seat beside her. Sam started the engine, and as soon as she exited the car park, she flicked on the siren.

"Are you crazy? Do you think this trip warrants us risking our lives? Slow down, Sam."

"Close your eyes. I've got a bad feeling about this. Three times I've called her, and not once has she picked up. Even you have to admit that's strange, partner."

He threw his hands up in the air. "If you say so. I'll call the team and let them know what's going on, just in case." He rang the station. "Oliver, it's me. We're on our way over to see Davina. The boss has got a feeling that something is wrong because the woman hasn't got back to her... Yeah, we've got a full day ahead of us... Carry on where you left off yesterday. Do me a favour and check Davina's Facebook page...? Don't worry, I'll do it on my phone. We'll be in touch soon. Over and out."

"Over and out? You're nuts. Why couldn't he check her Facebook page?"

"His computer was warming up. Most of them need replacing in our office, you know that as well as I do."

"There's little hope of that happening anytime soon, not with the new government. Cuts, cuts, cuts, that's all we hear these days. And don't get me started on them stripping the poor pensioners of what they're entitled to."

"Okay, calm down. I wish I hadn't mentioned it now."

"We're better off keeping this a politics-free zone. The subject always winds me up."

"You and three-quarters of the population, and for what it's worth, I agree with you about what they did to the pensioners. There was a clip on FB... nope, not going there. You've already stated that you're determined to keep politics out of the car."

"Thanks, partner. And here's a piece of advice for you: with the rise in AI-produced clips, I wouldn't believe everything I see on social media."

"You have a point."

Five minutes later, Sam killed the siren at the top of Davina's road. "Keep an eye open for number thirty-nine."

"It should be on the right here. This is fifty-seven."

Sam drew into a parking space not far from what she suspected was Davina's house, and they exited the vehicle. She rang the bell, but the door remained unanswered. Sam decided to call Davina's number. She strained an ear and even opened the letterbox to listen. There, in the distance, she could hear the phone ringing. She stood upright and held her hand to her ear. "Did you hear someone cry for help?"

Bob frowned and shook his head. "No."

"I definitely heard someone, which I believe gives us the go-ahead to break down the door."

Bob pointed at his chest. "And that's down to me, is it?"

"Get on with it. Her life could be in danger."

Bob shoulder-charged the door close to the lock. It took several attempts until, finally, the door gave way. Sam stepped over her partner, who ended up facedown on the Minton-tiled floor.

"Davina, Davina, are you here?"

"I'm in here," the young woman whimpered.

"Quick, Bob. I think she's upstairs." Sam bolted up the stairs and into the bedroom at the front. She found a woman lying on the bedroom floor with a bloody gash on her head. Sam crouched beside her. "Davina, are you all right? Who did this to you?"

"I don't know. My head is spinning. I can't see you. Who are you? Why can't I see you?"

Sam pushed the hair out of Davina's eyes. "It's okay, you're safe. I'm DI Sam Cobbs. I left you a message on your phone to contact me. What happened?"

"I don't know. Someone attacked me and kept me prisoner. They went out the back way."

"What? When?"

"They heard you breaking down the door. The person warned me that they would return. Help me, please."

"Bob, get after them."

Her eager partner didn't need to be told twice. He thundered down the stairs and through the house.

"Can you move?"

Davina reached out a hand. "I'm not sure if I can get to my feet. Why can't I see? What's wrong with my eyesight?"

"I don't know. I think we should get you to the hospital ASAP."

Determination allowed Sam to assist Davina to her feet.

The woman swayed and reached out. Tears coursed down her cheeks. "Why can't I see?"

"It's probably because of the injury to your head. I've seen this before. It's probably temporary. We'll be at the hospital soon." Sam helped Davina out of the bedroom, guiding her with her voice and steering her back on course when Davina drifted slightly.

Thankfully, Bob returned and tore up the stairs to help her. "I'm here. What can I do?"

"Just be there. Make sure she doesn't trip and fall."

"If she does, she'll land on me."

Sam nodded but didn't have it in her to smile at him. She was too worried about Davina and the effect her blindness, whether temporary or not, was having on the poor woman. "Should I call your parents?"

"Yes, yes, please. I didn't know where my phone was. I put it down and couldn't remember where I'd put it, not until it started ringing. I was disorientated."

"Don't worry. I'll get Bob to find it in a moment. Let's get you downstairs and into the car first."

More crying, which turned into understandable sobs. "What did I do? Someone hurt me for no reason. Why? If this isn't temporary, how will I cope with living alone? I won't, I know I won't."

"Let's not think about that for now. We've reached the bottom. We're going to lead you out to the car now. I can manage, Bob. Go back inside and find her phone. While you're in there, can you call SOCO? They need to be here."

Bob nodded and raced back inside the house. "Here we go. You need to keep walking in a straight line now. The car is about twenty feet from us."

"I'm scared," Davina sobbed.

"I know. Please, hang in there."

Sam made it to the car. She held Davina upright with one hand and struggled to pull the back door open with the other. Task completed with surprising dexterity, Sam helped Davina slip into the back seat. "There you are. You're safe now."

"If my blindness persists, I don't think I'm ever going to feel safe again. Why me? Why would someone choose to deliberately hurt me?"

"I don't know, but we're going to find out. Stay there, I'm going to go back to the house. We'll secure it again before we leave." Sam hoped that was true after the damage Bob had caused when he'd broken down the door. "Shit! What a mess." She surveyed the doorframe.

"Yeah, sometimes I don't know my own strength. It was important for us to get in, though. How is she?"

"Scared shitless that she's going to lose her sight forever. Did you see anyone out the back?"

"No. There were a couple of neighbours having a chinwag out there. I asked them if anyone had come past. They both said no."

"How strange. Okay, we can deal with that later. What we need to do now is secure the door... unless I take her to the hospital and you wait here until SOCO arrive. Yes, that's what we'll do. I'd feel happier about it."

"Yep, it makes sense. I can get a patrol out here and cadge a lift with them, if necessary."

Sam patted him on the shoulder. "Thanks for understanding. I'll keep in touch, you know what it's like at the A and E these days, especially in Whitehaven."

"I'm sure you'll be able to overcome that."

"See you later."

"Just go, leave all this to me to sort out."

"I'm going." Sam ran back to the car. She could see Davina was still crying in the back seat. She stepped back, removed her phone from her pocket and rang Mr Baldwin. "Hello, sir. This is DI Sam Cobbs."

"Oh, hello, Inspector. Are you ringing to tell us you've caught the killer?"

"No, I'm sorry. I'm calling to tell you that I'm on the way to A and E with Davina."

"What? No, don't tell me that someone has tried to kill her as well?"

"We're not sure what's happened yet. Umm... I'm very worried about her; she's telling me she can't see."

"Oh my God. We'll come to the hospital."

"Thank you. We should be there in about twenty minutes or thereabouts."

"We'll meet you there. Please, please, take care of our daughter. She's all we've got."

"Don't worry, she's in safe hands. See you soon." Sam ended the call and entered the car. "It's me, Davina. How are you feeling?" It seemed a silly question, but one that came naturally in the circumstances.

"Lost and confused as to why someone would hold me hostage and hurt me. Do you know why?"

Sam started the engine and drew away from the kerb. "We're investigating an incident that happened at your sister's home."

"What the...? Is Helen all right? What type of incident?"

"There was a fire. I'm sorry to have to tell you that your sister was killed."

Sam watched Davina's reaction in the rearview mirror and saw the colour drain from her rosy cheeks. "No," she whispered. "Not Helen. I don't believe you."

"It's true. I tried contacting you to see if you could help us with our enquiries. We've already spoken to your parents. I've left several messages on your phone, reaching out to you."

"I didn't get them. Well, maybe they came through, but I wasn't aware."

"How did this person get in your house? Sorry, were they male or female?"

"I don't know. They were wearing a mask and spoke in an automated voice. So it was difficult to tell."

"Don't worry. Did they tell you what they wanted?"

"No, only that I was to keep quiet. They beat me several times. I feared for my life, so I did exactly what they told me to do. They didn't tell me what they wanted or why they were holding me against my will. Do you think it had something to do with Helen's death?"

"At this stage, that seems the most obvious explanation. I'm sorry you've been subjected to such a terrible ordeal. I've called your parents. They're going to meet us at the hospital."

"What did you tell them?" She wiped away her tears with the sleeve of her cardigan.

"Not much."

Sam pulled up outside the main entrance to the hospital. She put her sign on the dashboard reading, 'Police Officer on Duty', and then helped Davina out of the car. She glanced over at the main door; there was a wheelchair outside. "Can you stay there just for a second? I'll be right back."

"Please, don't leave me for long."

"I won't, I promise." She jogged over to the entrance, removed the brake from the wheelchair and steered it back towards the car. "Here you go. You have your own personal taxi for the journey. Hop in."

"I hate these things," Davina complained.

"It'll be easier, just for now."

Sam applied the brake once more and then eased Davina into the chair. "Comfortable?"

"Not really."

Sam cringed. She removed the brake and wheeled Davina through the main entrance. At the reception desk, she showed her ID to the young man sitting behind the counter. "DI Sam Cobbs. I was called to an address and found Davina with a head injury. Can someone help us ASAP, please?"

"I'm blind," Davina added.

"Yes, that's right. Although, her blindness is due to the blow she received to her head."

"Ah, I see. Okay, let me have a word with someone. I won't be long." He left his cubicle and returned with a woman wearing a two-piece light-blue suit.

"Hello, I'm Doctor Murray. How long have you been blind?"

"A few hours, I'm not sure. Someone was holding me hostage. They beat me over the head with something heavy. Please, please, you have to help me."

Doctor Murray rested a hand on Davina's shoulder. "Don't worry, we'll get you straight through to triage now and run some tests on you."

Davina's head slumped forward. "Thank you so much."

The doctor walked off, expecting them to follow. Sam quickly explained to the receptionist that Davina's parents were on their way and then upped her pace to catch up with the doctor.

"Wait in here. I'll be right back." She closed the curtain around them and left them.

"I feel in the way," Davina whispered. "As if people don't believe me."

Sam squeezed Davina's shoulder. "Don't worry, everyone is trying to do their best for you."

"How long will my parents be?"

"Depending on the traffic—about twenty minutes from when I called them. Try to remain calm."

"That's easy for you to say. You're not the one who is blind."

Sam struggled to find a suitable reply to that.

Moments later, the curtain drew back, and the doctor entered the cubicle once more. She thoroughly inspected Davina's eyes.

"The good news is that I can't see any permanent damage done to the retina, and nothing has been displaced from what I can tell. Therefore, I believe your eyesight should return once your body has got over the shock of being battered."

Davina broke down in tears. This time, her relief was obvious. "Thank you."

"It may take a few days. We're going to admit you. Run a few tests as you've suffered blows to your head. We'll keep a close eye on you in the meantime. How does that sound?"

"As much as I hate the thought of being in hospital, I think it makes sense to be here. Thank you, Doctor."

"I'll make the necessary arrangements for you. I'll be back soon."

Sam felt the need to hug Davina once the doctor left. "There, that's great news, isn't it?"

"I hope so, if she's right."

Footsteps sounded outside, and the curtain was drawn back again. "I've got someone to see you," the nurse said. She stepped back to reveal Mr and Mrs Baldwin.

"Who is it?" Davina asked.

"It's us, darling. Oh, Davina, who did this to you?" Linda Baldwin asked. She rushed forward to hug her daughter.

"I don't know, Mum. It was awful. I can't see. They took my sight from me."

"Oh, darling. Have you seen a doctor?" Linda took a step back so her husband could hug his daughter.

"Yes, they're going to admit me. She reckons my sight will return soon. I hope she's right. I don't think I'll be able to cope if I lose my eyesight permanently."

"I'm sure it won't come to that," her father added tautly. "She should be out of this chair; it's not needed. We can help her onto the bed. They'll probably wheel her through the hospital and up to the ward in that, instead of that blasted chair."

"I agree. Let's get you onto the bed, Davina." Sam hooked the young woman's arm through her own, and the nurse, who was still with them, helped Davina get on the bed.

"There you go. That's much better, isn't it?" the elderly nurse said. "Can I get you a hot drink?"

"No. Some water will do, thank you," Davina replied.

The nurse left, and Mr Baldwin shot a glance at Sam. "How was this allowed to happen?"

"I tried several times to contact Davina yesterday. There was no answer."

"Why didn't you answer, Davina? You're usually glued to that damn phone of yours."

"Because someone was holding me hostage. Why are you taking this out on me, Dad? You're always the same. Helen could never do any wrong in your eyes."

"Now, don't start, you two." Linda jumped in between them and held a hand up. "The inspector doesn't want to hear you bickering with each other. It doesn't matter, Davina is in the best place for her now. She will receive the care she needs to deal with... her temporary blindness."

Mr Baldwin faced Sam and demanded, "What are you doing about this?"

"Everything we can. My partner is back at Davina's house, waiting for the Scenes of Crime Officers to arrive. We'll go over the house with a fine-tooth comb, I promise you."

"You'd better, or I'll be having a chat with your senior officer."

"Now, Matthew, stop that!" Linda ordered. "We need to be grateful to the inspector for finding Davina and bringing her to the hospital."

Mr Baldwin heaved out a breath. "I suppose. Forgive me. In the circumstances, I'm sure you can appreciate how upset we are about this situation. It seems inconceivable that we might have lost both of our daughters within hours of each other."

"I can't believe Helen is gone. I was shocked when the inspector told me. She was such a sweetheart, always willing to do anything and everything to help out other people."

"That's exactly what we told the inspector," Linda said. She held her daughter's hand between both of hers. "You're safe. We have to be thankful for small mercies, darling. I'm sure your eyesight will return soon."

"And if it doesn't, Mum? What will I do then?"

Linda glanced over at her husband. His eyes widened, and he shook his head. "Then you'll have to come and live with us, won't you?"

Mr Baldwin glared at his wife, threw back the curtain and left the cubicle.

"Who's that?" Davina asked.

"No one, love. It's your dad. He's gone to get some fresh air. You know how much he struggles dealing with stressful situations."

"Only too well. Thank you for the offer, Mum. It would be nice to come and stay with you for a little while to recuperate, even if my eyes do get better."

"You know you're welcome anytime, love."

"It hasn't always been the case. I know Dad thinks I'm a pest. People are different. I didn't want to be like Helen growing up. I know that pissed him off."

"Hush now. He's fine. We're both still devastated by the loss of Helen. Just be patient with him, that's all I ask, Davina."

"I will, Mum. Hopefully, our relationship will grow from strength to strength in the future."

"Let's hope so. It's been a long time coming, darling. Why don't you close your eyes and try to get some rest now?"

Davina wiggled to get comfortable and closed her eyes.

Sam and Linda left the cubicle and drew the curtain closed once more. They took a few steps away.

"I'm sure she'll be okay, Linda," Sam assured her.

"I know she will. They were so different. Helen was so far laid-back that she was almost horizontal. Whereas Davina, well, she has always tested the boundaries with us. Has driven her father to distraction most of her life."

"That's a shame. My sister and I are different, yet very similar at the same time, if that makes sense. We're mostly on the same page."

"It's something we've learned to live with over the years. What's going on, Inspector? Why have both my daughters been attacked? Have you discovered anything during your investigation?"

Sam was caught in a dilemma. Did she tell Linda that Helen was having an affair, or even that she was pregnant, or leave well alone for now? After a few seconds of soul-searching, she replied, "We're still trying to trace all of Helen's friends to see what they can tell us. At this stage, we haven't really uncovered anything, as such." She felt several pimples rise on her tongue.

"I suppose it is very early days yet. I still can't believe she's gone.

I've reached for my phone to call her several times since you left us. And now we have this to contend with, too. Poor Davina, she must have been upset when she heard the news about Helen."

"She seemed shocked when I told her. I would have thought that you'd have contacted her by now."

Linda's eyes widened. "Believe me, I tried several times to call her yesterday. Frustratingly, she ignored my calls. There's nothing new about that. Of course, I didn't know that she was in trouble at the time. I feel guilty for not popping around to see her. The thought didn't cross my mind. What a terrible position we find ourselves in. We're grateful to you for saving Davina. I dread to think what might have happened if you hadn't discovered her."

Sam shrugged. "It's all part of the service. My partner and I called around on the off-chance. We knocked on the door, and when there was no answer, I rang Davina's mobile. My concern escalated when I heard it ringing and she didn't answer it. I instructed my partner to break down the door, and we searched the house until we found her."

Linda gasped and covered her mouth with her hand. She dropped it to ask, "Was there anyone else in the house?"

"No, she told us the person holding her hostage had run out the back when they heard us breaking down the door."

"And you lost them?"

"My partner ran out the back door, but he couldn't see anyone. There were a couple of neighbours talking out there, but neither of them saw anyone."

"How strange. What if this person was still in the garden? Maybe they were hiding in the shed or something."

"It's a possibility. Our main priority was checking on Davina, ensuring she was okay. We helped her to her feet. I thought it would be quicker to put her in the car and drive her here, rather than wait for an ambulance to arrive."

"Thank you. I think I would have done the same. The paramedics are under so much stress these days, aren't they?"

"Unfortunately."

"What about Jason? Have you seen him?"

Sam frowned. "Not since yesterday. May I ask why?"

"He hasn't contacted us. We've not heard a single word from him. We welcomed that man into our lives and, when our daughter, his wife, died, we heard nothing. Do you think that's normal?"

"No. However, people deal with grief and the loss of a loved one in different ways. He was away at the time of the fire. I should imagine he feels guilty for not being there for Helen. He's lost everything: his wife and his home."

"He's not the only one. Other families stick together during times such as this. I don't think I will be able to forgive him for keeping his distance from us."

"Please, everyone is suffering from the loss of Helen, don't do anything rash."

Matthew returned, and he wrapped an arm around his wife. "Is everything all right here?"

"Yes. I was telling the inspector that Jason hadn't called or visited us. Her advice is to excuse his behaviour because he's probably grieving."

"Each to their own, eh? We'll do things our way. It wouldn't bother me if I never saw him again. I blame him for this. He should have been there for her."

Sam felt the walls closing in on her with no escape. The last thing she needed or wanted was to cause friction between husband and wife. "Maybe it's best not to concern yourselves with the way Jason is reacting and to concentrate your efforts on your other child. Davina is going to need your support for the next few days."

"And we intend giving it to her, don't we, dear?" Linda said. She shrugged off her husband's arm and went back into the cubicle to be with her daughter.

Matthew paced the corridor, his gaze flitting between Sam and the curtain shielding his daughter from him.

"Are you okay, Mr Baldwin?"

He swallowed and shook his head. "My life will never be the same again, not without Helen. She was so much more than a daughter to me. My heart has ached nonstop since we lost her. A deep, searing pain that I can't get rid of. Linda doesn't understand. Father and daughter relationships are so special."

Sam smiled. "I know. I'm very close to my father. That's not to say I wasn't close with my mother before she passed."

"I'm glad you understand." He came to a standstill in front of her and leaned in to say, "I shouldn't be telling you this, but my relationship with Davina has always been strained. She was a troubled teenager. Rebellious isn't the correct word. She was far worse than that. The thing is, she only acted that way with me, never with her mother."

"Maybe things will improve between you once her eyesight returns," Sam suggested.

"And if it doesn't?"

Sam struggled to find a suitable response to appease him.

The doctor arrived, along with a porter. They whisked Davina to triage, leaving Sam pacing the floor with her parents until she was returned or moved to a ward.

After waiting ten minutes, Sam took a punt and asked her parents, "There is one thing we've stumbled across during our investigation."

"What's that?" Linda was the first to ask.

"Does the name Brian Hanson mean anything to either of you?"

Matthew reached out to hold his wife's hand. "Yes, we know him. Why? Are you telling us he's responsible for killing our daughter?"

Raising her hand to prevent that thought, Sam replied, "No, he's just a person of interest, someone we'd like to speak with. May I ask how you know him?"

"Helen and Brian used to go out with each other," Linda said.

"Oh, I see. Can you remember how long the relationship lasted?"

"Gosh, now you're asking. Maybe eighteen months to two years."

"And when would that have been?"

"Just before she started going out with Jason," Linda replied.

"I believe that's why the relationship ended," Matthew said. "Because she started seeing Jason behind Brian's back."

"That makes sense."

"Why is he of interest to you?" Matthew demanded.

"We have footage of him having what appears to be a disagreement with Helen at Muncaster Castle."

"What? They argue and, on the same day, our daughter is killed. I'd call that more than just a coincidence, Inspector, wouldn't you?"

"Yes, that's why we're regarding him as a person of interest."

"Then why are you waiting around here? You should be out there, searching for the bastard," Matthew insisted, the anger in his voice obvious.

"I was concerned about your daughter. I was on my way to see Brian but veered off at the last minute to pay Davina a visit."

"You did the right thing," Linda said. She hooked her hand through her husband's arm. "Please, don't blame Sam. If she hadn't shown up at Davina's, our daughter wouldn't be receiving treatment right now."

"Okay, I understand that, but there's no reason for her to hang around now, is there? Not now that we're here."

Sam nodded. "That's fine. I've got what I needed to know about. I'll check in with Davina later, then. Take care." With that, she left the area and ran back to her car. She drove back to Davina's house to pick up Bob.

He was outside the property, checking his watch as she pulled up. "You took your time."

"Don't start, I've already had a pig of a day as it is. How long have SOCO been here?"

"About half an hour. They told me to keep out of the house because I didn't have a protective suit, and they refused to give me one of theirs. The bastards."

"They've been told to cut back, like all of us. Sorry, I should have left you one. I was too concerned about getting Davina to the hospital."

"Whatever, it's done now. How did you get on? Is her blindness temporary or permanent?"

"The good news is that the doctor seemed to believe it's temporary."

"Phew. I've never seen anything like that before. I suppose it depends on which part of the head the person strikes. Let's hope she regains her sight soon." He rubbed his hands together and blew on them. "Bloody freezing out there. Any chance we can stop off and have a coffee somewhere?"

"For you, anything."

Out of the corner of her eye, Sam saw his head turn to face her.

"Sometimes I can't tell if you're being sincere or sarcastic."

She sniggered. "I was being sincere that time around, and for the record, I enjoy keeping you on your toes."

"You do that all right."

Sam drove to one of the regular cafés and treated Bob to a bacon roll and a flat white. While she drank her coffee, she revealed what Davina's parents had told her about Brian Hanson.

Bob finished his mouthful of bacon roll, then said, "Wow, well then, there you go, he's got to be our top suspect now, hasn't he?"

Sam wagged a finger. "Hold your horses, big man. You're forgetting one vital clue."

He frowned and prepared to take another bite of his roll. "Which is?"

"The person seen lurking on the corner."

"They don't know who it is. We don't know for definite until we see for ourselves in any footage that is likely to surface."

"We need to chase that up with the team." She rang the station and spoke to Claire. "It's me. Has any footage been found from around the crime scene yet?"

"Yes, we've managed to track down a couple of door cam images, but they're very grainy, and all we can see is the outline of a person standing at the end of the road. It was pitch-black, which doesn't help either, boss."

"Damn. Okay, maybe we should send it over to the lab, see what they can do with it."

"I'll get that organised right away. How are things going with you?"

"Hit and miss. Davina is in hospital. We had to—sorry, correction, only because my partner is glaring at me over his bacon roll—*Bob* had to break down the door to her house. We found her just coming around. Someone had battered her with a heavy object and knocked her out. Not only that, but she told us they had held her hostage for a day, too."

"Oh shit! Is she all right?"

"Yes, the person ran off when we got there. Bob gave chase, but it was too late. They got away. Here's the worst thing about this: Davina was left blinded by the assault."

"Oh no, how dreadful. Can the doctors do anything for her?"

"The doctor seems to think it's temporary and is admitting her to keep an eye on her. Ouch, excuse the pun, it truly wasn't intended."

Bob groaned, and she stamped on his foot.

"Anyway, I left Bob at the house, and SOCO kicked him out into the cold, so we're having coffee and a bacon roll. Afterwards, we're going to go over to Brian Hanson's address. If he's not there, we'll shoot around to where he works at Wayland Electrics. Actually, scratch that, he's more likely to be at work at this time of the day. We'll take a gamble and stop there first. How are things going there?"

"Slowly, boss. I've been digging deep into Jason's past, his bank accounts and SM accounts, and nothing is showing up."

"Okay, we'll give it one more day and then move on from that. Maybe there's nothing to uncover, but thanks for trying to find something, Claire. Oh, and I forgot to mention that Helen's parents told me she and Brian used to be an item until she ditched him to go out with Jason."

"Very interesting. I'll go through his SM accounts, see if I can pick up his mood via his posts, if he's made any lately."

"Thanks. Also, check back ten years, around the time he broke up with Helen."

"Consider it done, boss."

"After we've dropped by to see Brian, we're going to swing by and have a chat with Vanessa as well."

"You have a busy morning ahead of you."

"We do. See you later." Sam ended the call.

"What did she say?"

"The footage they've got to hand is very grainy. She's going to send it to the lab and ask them to clean it up for us."

"And? Anything else?" he asked, narrowing his eyes.

"You know full well what she had to say. You could hear our conversation."

He grinned and pushed his empty plate to the side of the table. "I told you, Jason is clean. He couldn't—no, he would never—sink so low as to kill his wife and leave himself homeless."

Sam held her hands up and glanced around them. "Keep your voice down. We're in a public area."

"Sorry. But I'm right, why won't you admit it?"

"Because I can't. We're still sifting through all the evidence, Bob, so stop having a go at me for doing my job."

"Doesn't my word count? It doesn't appear to, not during this investigation. Or it hasn't so far."

She sucked in a breath and let it out slowly before she answered him. "It does. The team and I are ensuring we dot all the I's on this one first, that's all. I repeat, I value your judgement, always, all I'm doing is ensuring we don't blame the wrong person for a serious crime. As I always do during an investigation."

"Hmm... okay. I believe you." He emptied his cup and stood. "Are you ready?"

Sam hurriedly downed the rest of her drink and followed him out of the café, bidding the owner farewell on the way out. "We'll see you soon."

Sam and Bob entered the warehouse unit of the electrical company where Brian Hanson worked and spoke to the receptionist.

Sam produced her ID. "Hi, I'm DI Sam Cobbs. Is it possible to have a chat with Brian Hanson, please?"

The woman seemed taken aback by the suggestion. "Oh, right. Let me have a word with the boss. Just a moment."

She walked around the counter and knocked on the door to their left, which had a *Manager* plague on it. Her boss beckoned her in, and she closed the door behind her. She came out a few seconds later, followed by her boss.

"Hello. I'm Stan Bowles, the manager. I hear you want to speak with a member of my staff. Can I ask what it's concerning?"

"It's a personal matter."

"Then he can come and see you during his lunch hour or after work."

Sam shrugged. "If you insist."

"What's he done? I knew he was a bad 'un when I offered him the job, but he swore to me that he'd cleaned up his act and was on the straight and narrow these days."

"He hasn't *done* anything, as far as we're aware. We're investigating a serious crime and making enquiries, that's all."

"What serious crime? If it's serious and you want to have a word with him, then I'm entitled to know what's going on. I pay the man's salary, for God's sake."

"I can't tell you more than that at this time. Now, will you allow us to speak with him?"

His chest rose and fell as his anger grew. "Outside, off the premises. Go round the back, you can talk to him there."

"Thank you, much appreciated, because we have several other people we need to visit today."

The manager went back into his office and slammed the door.

"Charming!" Bob chuntered and walked towards the door.

"I'm sorry about him. He can be a real grouchy bugger at times," the receptionist said.

"Don't worry, we meet all sorts in our line of work. The entrance to the rear is on the left or right?"

She pointed to the right.

"Thanks for your help," Sam said and left the unit to catch up with her partner. "Oi, you. Calm down."

He flicked his hand. "Arseholes like that wind me up. Why can't people be civil when they talk to the police? We're only doing our job."

"I wonder how many coppers have uttered those words over the years. It doesn't matter, Bob. We've spoilt his day by showing up, wanting to speak with an employee he's given a second chance to. He's bound to be narked about it. Ignore it and move on."

"Your trouble is that you always see the best in people."

She laughed. "If that's my only flaw, then so be it. Come on, let's get this over with."

In the yard at the rear of the building, several men were standing around chatting, while two other men were in the process of loading up one of the vans. Sam and Bob approached the crowd.

Sam showed her ID. "We're looking for Brian Hanson. Is he here?"

The men standing around chatting pointed to one of the men loading up the van.

Sam and Bob crossed the yard towards the van. She hadn't recognised Brian from the image because he'd had his back to her. She tapped him on the shoulder.

"What the fu... who are you? You scared the shit out of me."

"You might want to control that language of yours in front of a lady, mate," Bob advised.

"Sorry. You scared me. We don't often get members of the public round here. Who are you?" he repeated, his gaze taking in Sam's figure.

"DI Sam Cobbs, and this is my partner, DS Bob Jones. We've spoken to your boss; he's cleared us to have a chat with you."

He prodded his chest with his finger and glanced over Sam's shoulder at all of his colleagues watching them. "Me? Why me? What have I done?"

"Is there somewhere we can go?"

"Inside. Yes, this lot are nosey effers; I can do without this hassle. I ain't done nothing wrong, not in years. My bird would kick me out if I went back to my old ways."

"Glad to hear it. After you."

He put the last box in the back of the van, then they followed him inside the warehouse to the far corner, away from prying eyes and ears. "Go on then, tell me what this is about."

"Can you confirm you were at Muncaster Castle yesterday?"

"I can. I was helping out a friend who was exhibiting her cakes there. Her husband was taken ill, and I stepped in at the last minute."

"That was kind of you. So you took the day off work to help your friend?"

"No, I had booked a day off because I went to the dentist first thing. What does my being there have to do with anything?"

"Did you bump into anyone at the castle? Anyone from your past?"

"You know damn well I did, so why are you beating around the bush? Just come out and say it."

"We've caught the discussion you had with your former girlfriend on camera."

He scratched the back of his head and appeared puzzled. "So what? I met up with Helen. It's the first time I've seen her in years. She stuck her nose up in the air as soon as she saw me and pretended she didn't know me. It got under my skin, so I tackled her about it. You'd do the same if someone treated you like that, wouldn't you?"

"I'm not sure I would, especially if I broke up with them years ago."

"Well, that's because you and I are different. She's a snobby cow these days; she wasn't like that when she was with me. It got my back up, and I decided to have it out with her."

"And how did the conversation go?"

"She denied treating me like shit. Told me she was very busy and that she didn't have time to spend arguing the toss with me. I told her to F off and that was the end of it. If you're here because she's told you something different, then she's a frigging liar. She's changed, and not for the better, either. She has no right looking down her nose at me, no right at all."

"Calm down, there's no need for you to become angry. All we're doing is conducting enquiries into an incident that was caught on camera between you and Helen."

"With the aim of what?"

She chewed her lip and pondered whether to reveal the truth behind their visit.

"Why are you stalling? What the hell is going on here?"

"The reason we're here is because Helen was killed yesterday."

His head jutted forward, and his jaw dropped. Regaining his composure, he asked, "She what? How did she die?"

"Someone assaulted her, and her home was set on fire. We believe it was arson."

"No, no, no... you're not telling me that you think I had something to do with this, are you?"

"Possibly. As I've already stated, we're following up on a line of enquiry that has come our way."

He faced the wall and bashed his clenched fists against it. "This is utter bullshit. I had nothing to do with the fire. For a start, I don't even know where she lives, so how could I possibly go there and torch it?"

"When was the last time you saw each other before you saw her at the castle?"

"What? It's been about ten years. She dumped me to go out with that tosser, Jason. Last I heard, they got married not long after. Good luck to them. They were both cheating shits. He was dating a girl at the time, too. No loyalty, either of them. I've never cheated on anyone. I don't believe in it. Have the decency to end a relationship before you start seeing someone else; that's always been the way with me. Jesus, I can't believe you're standing here telling me that my ex is dead and that you think I'm the cause of her death. I want a lawyer. This ain't right."

"There's no need for that. All the footage proves is that you had words with Helen. I believe you when you tell us that you don't know where she lives."

"Good, because it happens to be the truth. I'm sorry she's dead. Are you sure it wasn't an accident?"

"No, the fire was deliberately started. We have the evidence we need. All we have to do now is find out who was responsible."

"Well, I can categorically tell you it wasn't me. I'm with someone I love now. I didn't like the woman she had become, but that doesn't mean to say that I would intentionally set out to harm her. So you're barking up the wrong tree coming here accusing me of all sorts. I've done nothing wrong."

"We weren't insinuating you had. However, I'm sure even you would agree that it would be wrong of us to dismiss the evidence we have of you and Helen arguing."

He leaned against the wall, tipped his head back and bashed his skull against it. "How many times do I have to tell you? I had nothing to do with this fire or killing Helen. It was a chance meeting, and I let rip at her. I regret doing it." He bounced off the wall and held his arms out to the sides. "Don't tell me you've never vented your anger at an ex before."

Sam shook her head. "I haven't. Have you, Sergeant?"

"Nope, I can't say I have."

"If you're intent on blaming me for this, then what else can I say?"

"You can tell us where you were two nights ago," Sam asked.

"That's easy. I was down my local all night, involved in a snooker tournament."

Bob removed his notebook from his pocket. "What's the name of the pub?"

"The Three Arrows in Schoose. It's at the end of my road, within staggering distance. That's why my girlfriend and I chose the house. And she was there with me. So feel free to give her a call."

"Is she at work now?"

"No, she's in between jobs at the moment. She was seriously ill a few months ago, and her boss sacked her for taking too much time off work."

"I'm sorry to hear that. Is she better now?"

"She's getting there. I could give her a ring if you want me to."

Sam nodded. "Great."

He withdrew his phone from the back pocket of his jeans and punched in his passcode. "Hi, May. I've got someone who wants to talk to you. She can tell you who she is."

"Hi, May. Sorry to disturb you. I'm Detective Inspector Sam Cobbs of the Cumbria Constabulary."

"What? The police? Oh God, what's he been up to? He promised me he had changed his ways. Shit... I can't deal with this, not now... not after the chemo I've been through."

"Stop, please, let me speak. I'm calling to ask you where Brian was two nights ago."

"He was with me at the pub. We attended a snooker tournament. Why?"

"That's all we need to know. Thank you."

"Wait, stop. You have to tell me what this is about."

"We have to get on. I'll pass the phone back to Brian. He can fill you in." Sam smiled and handed the phone back. "Thanks for speaking with us and for allowing us to talk with May. I've heard enough. We won't be bothering you any more."

"Thank God for that. Just because I've had a record in the past, you shouldn't leap all over people. Some of us choose to change, you know."

"To be honest, we weren't aware of your record. It was seeing your confrontation with Helen on the footage which brought us here."

He shrugged and walked back through the warehouse. Sam and Bob followed.

"I'm glad you believed me, and I'm really sorry Helen is dead."

"Thanks for being so understanding."

"I guess you were just doing your job. I hope you find who you're looking for."

"So do we."

Sam and Bob headed back to the car.

"I thought things were going to become sticky there for a moment or two," Bob muttered while they were still within earshot of the men in the yard.

"You're not the only one."

"So, where does that leave us?"

Sam pointed her key fob at the car and unlocked the doors. "We'll discuss it inside." She opened the driver's door and slipped behind the steering wheel. "We've still got Vanessa to interview. I need to do something first." She withdrew her phone from her pocket and rang the station. After being patched through to her team, she asked to speak with Oliver.

"Yes, boss?"

"Are you busy?"

"Not really. We're going through Jason's background information and SM accounts. What do you need me to do?"

"I'd like you and Liam to nip over to Davina's house. Check with the neighbours and ask if they've seen anyone hanging around or if anyone saw the person who was holding Davina hostage and assaulted her yesterday."

"Ah, right. We can shoot over there now. I'll check if there are any cameras in the area, too."

"I was about to suggest the same. Bob didn't see anyone when he checked out the back and asked a couple of neighbours chatting out there at the time. They told him they hadn't seen anyone go past. There's a possibility that the suspect might have still been in the garden, maybe hiding behind the shed or something until Bob returned to the house."

"I'm with you. We'll head over there now."

"Good luck. I'll check in with the hospital again once we've interviewed Vanessa. By the way, we can scrub Brian Hanson off the suspect list."

"Makes sense, considering Helen's neighbour said she thought she saw someone hanging around just before the fire was started."

"Indeed. We'll return to base after we've spoken to Vanessa." Sam ended the call and started the engine. "I think everything has been covered now; feel free to shout out if you believe I've missed anything."

"I don't think you have. This is turning out to be a frustrating case, isn't it?"

"You're not wrong. It's knowing who to visit and which way to turn first. Let's hope we get somewhere with Vanessa."

"How are you going to handle her?"

"Meaning?"

"Well, we both know she was having an affair with Jason. Are you going to question her about that from the outset or what?"

"I'm not sure. I'd prefer to see what kind of reception she gives us first. Jason has probably been in touch with her and maybe warned her that we will most likely be showing up on her doorstep."

"You're probably right."

SAM DREW to a halt in the car park at the rear of Trowbridge Financial Consultants, and they walked around the side to the front of the property. Three people were sitting at their desks: two men and a woman. Sam smiled as the woman approached the counter.

"Hello, how may I help you?"

Sam showed her warrant card. "DI Sam Cobbs and DS Bob Jones. Is it possible to speak with Vanessa Mitchell?"

"Oh, the police. Vanessa is with a client at present. Do you want to wait or call back? She shouldn't be too long, and she doesn't have another appointment booked until this afternoon."

"Thanks. We'll wait."

"Can I get you a drink?"

"That's kind of you. Two coffees, white with one sugar, thanks."

"I take two in mine," Bob reminded her.

"Sorry, one with two sugars," Sam called after the receptionist.

They took a seat in the comfy chairs, and Sam picked up a *Homes and Garden* magazine. She flicked through it until something of interest caught her eye. "This is a beautiful garden."

"Abigail would love something that big. Me, I just see a lot of hard work. She wouldn't be up for that. It would land on my shoulders, and I'm lacking in the green fingers department."

"You're not alone there. Thankfully, when Rhys moved in, he took over caring for the garden, mowing the lawn and tending to the plants. It was a wilderness before he started knocking it into shape. He finds it therapeutic being out there after work or at the weekends."

"I suppose it's different if you're stuck in an office all day, like he is."

"Yeah, I never thought about it that way before. I'm glad he's keen, saves me a job." She grinned and continued to flick through the pages until the receptionist arrived with their drinks.

"I found a couple of shortbread biscuits for you."

"Thank you. It's much appreciated."

The receptionist smiled and returned to her desk.

Sam and Bob had almost finished their drinks when two people rounded the corner ahead of them. The woman wore a pale-lilac suit and had long blonde hair. She was laughing with a man who was shorter than her. She showed him to the front door and opened it for him.

"I'll be in touch soon, Mr Woods. Be sure to say hello to your wife for me and wish her a speedy recovery."

"Thank you, Vanessa, for putting up with useless old me. Jemima is so well-versed in our accounts. I'm glad you made sense of it all in the end."

"We sorted it. That's all that matters. I'll run some figures on the computer and get back to you by the end of the day. Take care."

"You too. Thanks again."

The man stepped out of the building, and Vanessa closed the door. It was then that she noticed Sam and Bob.

"Are you waiting to see me?" Her gaze drifted over to the receptionist, who confirmed who they were. "The police? You'd better come through to my office. Would you like another drink?"

"No, thanks, we're fine," Sam said.

She and Bob got to their feet and followed Vanessa to her office. It was nicely decorated with an antique desk and matching filing cabinets. A row of bookshelves lined one wall, while a window on the other side overlooked a pretty courtyard filled with various-sized pots containing a variety of shrubs.

"Please, take a seat. What may I do for you?"

"Thank you for seeing us. We're investigating a serious crime that took place two nights ago."

Vanessa kept her gaze locked on Sam and reached for her pen. She twiddled it through her fingers. "Oh, what type of crime?"

"An arson attack."

"Oh dear. Where?"

"Here's the thing. We believe you know the property owners."

Vanessa frowned. "I do? Who are you talking about?"

"Helen and Jason Flintoff."

Nothing. Vanessa gave no reaction to the names at all.

"You do know them, don't you?"

"I've met Mr Flintoff once or twice at some networking events that I've attended over the years. What does this have to do with me?"

Sam smiled. "Ah, well, we've been told that you know Jason better than you're admitting."

Vanessa's cheeks flushed. "What's he told you?"

"Is he more than a mere acquaintance to you?"

She dropped the pen and ran a hand over her face. "Yes. We've been seeing each other for months."

"Thank you for being honest with us. Where were you the night before last?"

"I was in Carlisle... with Jason."

"Alone?" Sam asked.

"No, we were on a course together at the Crest Hotel."

"Were you sharing a room?"

She nodded, and tears welled up in her heavily made-up eyes. "Yes. I didn't know about the fire."

"I find that incredibly hard to believe that Jason hasn't contacted you."

"He hasn't. I swear he hasn't. He left early the following morning. I've tried to contact him several times, but he's refused to pick up the phone and hasn't returned my messages." She gasped. "Oh no, you're not telling me he was hurt in the fire, are you? I've been going out of my mind, not being able to contact him."

"No, he wasn't hurt in the fire, but his wife was."

"What? Is she okay?"

Sam raised an eyebrow. "Why the sudden concern for the woman who is married to your lover?"

"I never meant to hurt her."

"Sorry? What do you mean by that?"

"Our affair. It just happened. We were both lonely."

"And you fell into bed with each other at one of these networking events, is that correct?"

"You make it sound so sordid. It wasn't like that at all. We found it hard to resist each other. It didn't take us long to realise that we had feelings for each other."

"If that's the case, why do you think Jason hasn't contacted you?"

She shook her head, and fresh tears slipped down her cheeks. "How should I know? I'm going to call him, see what's going on, if I can get him to answer."

"By all means."

Vanessa picked up her iPhone and punched in her passcode, then dialled a number. She put the phone on speaker and placed it on her desk until Jason's voicemail kicked in. "See, I told you. I haven't been able to contact him since he left the hotel. He refused to tell me where he was going. I had no idea there was a fire at his home. I'm perplexed as to why he wouldn't tell me. You didn't answer me when I asked about his wife. Is she all right?"

"No. Helen is dead. Someone killed her and then set fire to her home."

"She's what? I don't believe you."

"Why would I lie? I'm not in the habit of lying, Miss Mitchell, especially in such dire circumstances. Can I look at your phone, please?"

Vanessa stopped sobbing. She snatched her phone off her desk and held it to her chest. "Why?"

"There's something I need to check."

"No. It's mine. You have no right asking to see my personal property."

"Okay. Have it your way. I think it would be better if you accompanied us to the station."

"Why? No, I haven't done anything wrong. You can't do this?"

"We're quite within our rights if we suspect you of committing a serious crime."

"What? Do you think I started the fire? That's bullshit. I wasn't even in the area. I refuse to come with you."

"If you don't come with us, then we'll have no alternative but to arrest you. Which is it to be?"

"I want to call my solicitor."

"By all means. You can do that from the station."

Sam and Bob both stood.

Vanessa stared at Sam. "You've got this all wrong."

"We'll see. Do you need to take your bag with you?"

"Jesus Christ, how has it come to this? All I did was sleep with Jason. I swear I've done nothing else."

"You can have your say under caution, back at the station."

She placed her arms on the desk and rested her head on them, then sobbed. Sam found the scene to be quite overdramatic, given the circumstances.

"Delaying the inevitable won't help, Vanessa. We can call your solicitor on the way."

Vanessa shot upright and swiped the tears from her flushed cheeks. "You think this is all an act, don't you? It's not. I'm appalled that you should come here and accuse me of killing someone."

"I haven't, not yet. I'm trying to get to the bottom of who killed your lover's wife. Taking the mistress in for questioning seems the most logical step, wouldn't you agree?"

"No, I wouldn't. Because I've already told you that I was nowhere near the scene; I was over fifty miles away. Why won't you believe me? I know, you can call the hotel, ask them what time I checked out."

"We'll do that, don't worry. Are you ready to go?"

Her hands gripped the arms of her chair, and she vehemently shook her head. "No."

"Okay, you leave me no alternative but to arrest you. Put the cuffs on her, Sergeant."

Sam proceeded to read Vanessa her rights while Bob tussled with the woman to get to her wrists. Vanessa started screaming for help.

The door burst open, and the two men who were in the outer office barged into the room. Sam was prepared for them. She thrust her warrant card in their faces.

"Back off. She's overreacting. We're within our rights to take her in for questioning."

"For what?" one of the men asked, clearly aghast that Vanessa was still putting up a fight.

"Suspected arson."

"I haven't done anything. It's a pack of lies. Don't listen to her. Call my solicitor, Greg Davidson. His number is in my address book on my desk."

One man ran towards the desk and snatched her address book. He flicked through the pages, then made the call.

Ignoring him, Sam tried to assist Bob, who had managed to hook his cuffs on one of Vanessa's wrists. She lashed out and beat him with her other fist.

"Stop it, Vanessa. You're only making things worse for yourself."

"I'm innocent, and you're trying to arrest me for something I haven't done."

Sam got hold of the woman's flailing arm. She held it still long enough for Bob to slap the other cuff on. Vanessa let out a harrowing scream that made Sam's ears ring.

"Don't let them take me, Andy and Carl, please?"

Both men shrugged. "It's out of our hands. Your solicitor is on his way to the station. He told me to tell you to remain calm. He'll get it sorted when he arrives. Vanessa, go with the officers. You're only going to make it worse for yourself if you don't."

"But I'm innocent. I haven't done anything wrong. You have to believe me."

"Calm down," Bob warned.

Vanessa screamed again and then passed out.

"What the hell," Bob muttered.

"You can't take her, not when she's passed out on you. I'm calling for an ambulance," Andy said.

"No, don't do that. Get me a glass of water," Sam ordered.

Carl took off and returned with the water, which he handed to Sam. She didn't hesitate and threw it in Vanessa's face.

The woman spluttered to life. "What the hell is going on? Why did you do that to me?"

"You passed out or pretended you had. It's the easiest way to bring someone around."

"I'll get you for that," Vanessa sneered.

"Is that a threat, Miss Mitchell? If it is, I have three witnesses who heard you say it."

"Fuck off."

Sam smiled down at the woman. "On your feet, unless you want to add resisting arrest to the charges."

"Bollocks. You're a dumb copper if you believe I had anything to do with this."

"If you're innocent, you're going the wrong way about this, Vanessa. Now, are you going to behave and come with us, or will I have to Taser you? The choice is yours."

Vanessa growled through gritted teeth and stood. "My solicitor is going to wipe the floor with you. I'll make sure he does."

"Whatever. Thanks for your help, Andy and Carl. You can go back to work now. You might want to cancel Miss Mitchell's appointments for the rest of the day and possibly tomorrow as well."

Vanessa kicked off again. "What? There's no way I'm spending the night in a cell."

"We'll see."

Sam and Bob stood on either side of Vanessa and steered her through the doorway and out of the building. The receptionist had a hand over her mouth, shocked to see her boss being manhandled.

6

Upon their arrival, Vanessa's solicitor was waiting for them in the reception area. "Take those cuffs off. There's no need to treat her like a common criminal. Vanessa is a well-respected member of our community," Davidson shouted.

"We'll take them off in the interview room. Vanessa tried to resist arrest. The cuffs were placed on her for our safety."

"Vanessa, is this true?"

Vanessa inclined her head in shame, then raised it and said, "Only because I'm innocent. They refused to believe me, and this is the consequence. Greg, I swear to you, I have done nothing wrong. This has all been a terrible mistake. Please, help me."

"I will, don't worry. I need to have a private word with my client before the interview begins."

Sam nodded. "Of course." She turned to Nick and asked, "Is there an interview room free, Sergeant?"

"Number One is free, ma'am. Can I help at all?"

"No, Bob and I can manage. Follow us, Mr Davidson." Sam covered the number pad and inserted her security code. She led Vanessa and her solicitor down the hallway, while Bob brought up the rear. "We'll give you ten minutes." She closed the door on them, leaned against the wall and whispered, "That escalated quickly."

Bob bent over and rested his hands on his knees. "You're telling me. She's stronger than she looks. Stupid cow, it needn't have turned out like that."

"Correct. Which could mean that she's totally innocent."

"Or it could mean she's guilty as sin."

"Let's leave them to it and see how Claire is getting on."

They climbed the stairs and found Claire tapping away at her computer.

"How did it go, or shouldn't I ask?"

"Do we look that bad?" Sam crossed the room to check out her reflection in the mirror. Her hair was a mess, and her blouse was untucked. "Bugger, why didn't you tell me, Bob?"

"Er, can't say I'd noticed. She put up a hell of a fight, so I'm not surprised we look a mess."

"Sounds ominous. Is this Vanessa Mitchell you're talking about?"

"Yes," Sam replied. "She's swearing blind that she had nothing to do with the fire, although she has admitted that she was having an affair with Jason."

"That's a start, I suppose."

"Have Liam and Oliver reported in yet?"

"Not yet."

"And how are things going with you?"

"I seem to be chasing my tail a lot. I'll keep digging, though. I'm determined to find something of relevance."

Sam poured herself a glass of water and then walked towards the door. "Are you ready for round two, partner?"

"I might sit this one out. I'm still feeling the effects of the last battle I had with her."

She laughed. "Come on, it's you and me against the world, mate."

"Not what I wanted to hear," he complained and followed her out of the room.

Claire wished them good luck.

"We're going to need a bucketful of that," Bob said.

"Have faith. Her solicitor may have worked miracles and calmed her down."

"There again, the opposite might be true. Fancy having a wager?"

"Not really. You think she's going to go down the 'no comment' route, don't you?"

"Yep. I bet a month's salary on it."

"I think you're wrong." Sam inhaled a calming breath and then opened the door to the interview room.

"We haven't finished, Inspector."

"We've been more than fair and given you extra time for your consultation, Mr Davidson. We have a lot to get through, and time is marching on."

Sam and Bob sat in the seats on the other side of the table. While Bob said the necessary verbiage for the recording, Sam studied Vanessa, who had her gaze fixed on the wall behind Sam.

"Are you ready to talk now, Vanessa?" Sam asked.

"For your information, I answered all the questions you asked me in my office. Or have you forgotten that, Inspector?"

"Not all of them. We've had a look at your phone and can confirm our findings, which are that you sent Helen numerous messages. Why?"

She remained silent and glanced at Davidson for help.

He spoke for her. "Surely, if you have access to my client's phone, you're privy to the messages she sent."

"We are. Okay, if that's the way you want to play it. Miss Mitchell, why have you been pestering to see Helen Flintoff over the last three weeks?"

"I wanted to speak with her."

"I'm aware of that from the content of the messages. What I'm struggling to understand is why you would want to meet up with the woman whose husband you were, sorry, *are* sleeping with. Care to enlighten us?"

Vanessa's demeanour changed from being angry to submissive. Her chin dropped to her chest, and the tears started to fall again.

Sam watched her for several seconds without speaking, until her frustration became tighter than a guitar string. "Would you like me to repeat the question?"

"No, there's no need. I thought we needed to meet up and discuss things."

"What things? How many mistresses throw the gauntlet down to a man's wife, demanding that they meet?"

"I'm not like most women, I like to do things differently."

Sam detected an arrogance emerging that she was keen to counter. "Different to most women? In what way?"

"When I see what I want, I go after it."

Sam scratched the side of her face. "You're talking about Jason?"

Vanessa smiled and cocked an eyebrow. "That's right. We were making plans..."

"What sort of plans? To kill her?"

"What? Don't be so ridiculous. I would never sink that low, and neither would Jason."

"How can you be so sure... about Jason, I mean? How well do you really know the man you've been sleeping with behind his wife's back?"

"All right, there's no need for you to keep saying it that way. It wasn't the sordid affair you're making it out to be. We're very much in love."

"With another woman's husband. A woman who has been murdered this week, and yet, here you are, sitting opposite me with little or no remorse."

"Remorse? Why should I feel any remorse? I wasn't the one who was cheating on their partner, therefore, I have nothing to feel remorseful about."

Sam shook her head, anger searing her veins. "You don't feel bad that Helen is dead?"

"I didn't say that. You asked if I felt any remorse. I don't."

"As my client has already said, why should she feel any remorse? Affairs happen all the time. Sometimes love just happens between two people; we have to accept that, Inspector."

"Forgive me if I don't agree with that concept. What we're talking about here is your client. The mistress in this relationship is sitting here, trying to justify being in love with the victim's husband. Doesn't that seem rather odd to you? Or am I missing something?"

"Let's get to the point: it appears to me that what you're setting out to do is make my client slip up and admit that she killed Helen Flintoff."

"Not in the slightest, Mr Davidson. All I'm doing is searching for the truth, and I believe I'm looking at someone who is guilty of wrecking a marriage and possibly killing Helen Flintoff."

Vanessa sprang forward in her chair and bashed her fists on the table. "Give me a break. All I'm guilty of is sleeping with Jason, end of. I did not set fire to their home. I was fifty miles away in Carlisle, with Jason. I gave you that information in my office earlier. I also advised you to check my alibi with the hotel. Have you done that yet?"

"Not yet, all in good time."

"I think that should be carried out immediately before this interview goes any further," Davidson said.

"Very well." Sam nodded at Bob to announce her departure for the recording. She ran upstairs and asked Claire to look up the number for Crest Hotel in Carlisle.

Claire supplied the number, and Sam made the call from her office. "Hello, is it possible to speak with the manager?"

"Oh, yes. I think he's available. Who shall I say is calling?" the receptionist asked.

"DI Sam Cobbs from Workington."

"Hold the line."

Sam tapped her pen on the desk until a man came on the line.

"Hello, this is Edward Tindle, the manager. How may I help you?"

"Sorry to disturb you, Mr Tindle. I'm DI Sam Cobbs from the Cumbria Constabulary based in Workington."

"Okay. What do you need from me, Inspector?"

"I'm investigating a major crime in the area, and a couple of the witnesses have informed me that they were staying at your hotel the night of the incident. I'd like you to confirm that for me, if you wouldn't mind?"

"Of course. Let me pull up the bookings screen for you. What date are we talking about?"

"Two nights ago, so that would be the eleventh."

"Ah, yes. I have it here. The names you want me to check are? But first, I'm going to need proof that you're who you say you are."

"Of course. I'll send a copy of my ID now. Can you hold?"

"Yes. I'll give you the fax number."

Sam copied her ID and sent it via fax.

After a slight delay, the manager came back on the line. "Right, that seems all good to me. Now, where were we? Ah, yes, the first name you want me to look up?"

"Great. It's Jason Flintoff."

"Yes, he was in room 102. He left the next day, although he was originally booked for the week. I believe he was attending a course here at the hotel."

"Thanks, that confirms the information he told me. The second person is Vanessa Mitchell."

"Mitchell, Mitchell, ah, yes, here she is. She was booked into the room next door to him in 104."

"Can you tell me when she left the hotel?"

"I can. She also left the following day. I was in reception that day. She said she had an emergency at home that she needed to attend to."

"Can you recall what time she booked out?"

"Let me check that for you. Yes, it was ten-twenty-five."

"You've been very helpful, sir. I can't thank you enough."

"I pride myself on always helping the police wherever possible. Is there anything else, Inspector?"

"No, thanks very much."

"Then I will bid you a good day."

"Goodbye, sir."

Sam ended the call and glanced out of the window towards the hill. Her gaze dropped to a figure at the back of the car park, leaning against a car with the driver's door open. She collected her glasses from her desk to get a better look at the person and gasped. *Warren Goldman. What the fuck is he doing here?* Sam bolted out of the office and down the stairs.

"Is everything all right, boss?" Claire called after her.

"I don't know. I'll let you know later."

Nick asked the same question as she sped through the reception area to the outside. Warren spotted her approaching him and hurriedly slipped into the driver's seat.

Sam upped her pace, her heart frantically beating against her ribs. "Stop right there, Mr Goldman."

He didn't. Instead, he started his engine and revved it. Sam stood her ground and came to a halt three feet in front of the car.

She raised her hands and shook her head. "Don't do this. Get out of the car. I just want a quick chat with you."

He revved the engine more and inched forward until he was about a foot from Sam. She could see the anger contorting his features and, in that split second, she feared for her life.

A siren sounded behind her. Sam turned to find a patrol car blocking Warren's path. She waved to thank the officer for helping her then raced around the side of the vehicle and tore open the driver's door. "Do you mind telling me what you're doing here?"

"I wanted to see what was going on with the investigation."

"By threatening to run me over?"

"If that was my intention, I would have done it."

"Why are you here?"

He stared at the station ahead of him. "I saw you bring her in."

"Who?"

"That Vanessa woman."

Sam was shocked to learn the news. "Have you been following me?"

"No, er, maybe."

"Why?"

"Because I want to ensure you conduct the investigation thoroughly."

"Have I given you any reason to doubt my abilities? I'm a seasoned pro, Mr Goldman. At this moment, there's only one person around here raising my suspicions, and that's you."

"I haven't done anything wrong. All I'm doing is making sure these people don't pull the wool over your eyes."

"I assure you, they won't. My reputation over the past fifteen years speaks for itself. You shouldn't be here. In fact, I could arrest you for interfering with an investigation."

He jabbed a finger at his chest. "Me? I haven't done anything wrong—they have. They killed her."

"Who do you suspect?"

"That husband and that bitch of a mistress. I hope you've brought her in to turn the screws on her."

Sam smiled. "When we bring people in for questioning, we never resort to torturing them, I can assure you."

"Maybe you should consider it for some folks. I'm pleading with you not to listen to the lies they tell you. Helen told me she didn't trust them."

"You didn't tell me that. What else did Helen confide in you?"

"That she wanted to leave him. She was desperate to leave him."

"What? And be with you? Is that what you're telling me?"

"The conversation never cropped up. She had a mind of her own. I believe that baby was mine. Any news on the DNA test yet?"

"I can chase it up, but why punish yourself like that? What if it is yours? What's the point of knowing, if the baby is dead?"

He placed a hand over his heart. "I can feel it here. If the baby is mine, then I have a right to grieve its loss, just like any other father. It can't be his."

"Why can't Jason be the father?"

"Because Helen told me he was infertile."

Sam's eyes widened. "Are you telling me the truth?"

"Why would I lie to you about something so important?"

"Okay, then I'll check with the pathologist, ask him to do a DNA test for you. I'm going to need to take a sample from you first."

"Of course. Do you want me to come in?"

"Yes, park up and follow me inside. I'll have to leave you in the capable hands of the desk sergeant, though, because I need to continue interviewing Vanessa."

"Thank you for not taking further action against me. I wouldn't have knocked you down, I promise."

Sam closed the door and allowed him to park the car while she thanked her colleague in the patrol car and dismissed him.

Warren joined her, and they walked back into the reception area together.

"Nick, can you do me a favour and take a sample of DNA from Mr Goldman, please?"

"Right away, ma'am. Do you want me to send it over to the lab for you?"

"Yes, I'll give the pathologist a call now. Tell him to expect it." She faced Warren once more. "I'll leave you in the sergeant's capable hands and also issue you with a warning."

"About?"

"Backing off. Allow us to conduct the investigation without any further interference, otherwise I will be forced to arrest you. Am I making myself clear?"

"Yes, absolutely clear. I'm sorry. I never meant to cause you any trouble."

Sam patted his forearm and said, "My team and I will get to the truth. It's early days yet, but we haven't stopped searching for the truth."

"I'm sorry. It won't happen again."

"I hope not." She punched in her security code and left the reception area. On the other side of the door, she rang Des. "Hi, can you talk?"

"I can, fortunately for you. What's up?"

"I've just had a weird interaction with a man who was Helen's lover. I told him she was pregnant. He showed up at the station. Well,

I won't go into detail about what happened. The outcome of the situation is this: he believes the baby was his. So, I suggested carrying out a DNA test on the foetus. Did I cross the line?"

"No. I can arrange that for you if you send a sample over to me."

"I'm in the middle of interviewing the husband's lover at present. I've asked the desk sergeant to take the sample for me. He'll get one of his officers to drop it off at the lab."

"Marvellous. I'll let the techs know that it's on the way. We should have a result for you by the end of the day."

"That's what I was hoping you'd say. Thanks, Des."

"How's the investigation going?"

"Slowly. Lots of people to interview. We had a major incident to attend to yesterday."

"I'm listening and intrigued to hear."

"We called round to interview Helen's sister; we'd been trying to contact her since we spoke to her parents. When we got to the house, we had to break in because I sensed she was in trouble."

"Oh heck. Was she?"

"Yes, she told us that someone had held her hostage."

"What? When was this? At the same time as the fire was started?"

"We believe so, yes. That's not all. When we found her, she had been bashed over the head. The strike was powerful enough to make her lose her eyesight."

"Jesus, if that's the case, she was lucky to still be alive. Blows to the head can be life-threatening in my experience. Where is she now?"

"We rushed her to A and E, and the doctor insisted she wanted to keep Davina in for observation for a day or two."

"That's a wise decision. What are the chances of her regaining her eyesight?"

"The doctor seems to think it's temporary."

"That's a relief. Right, enough chitchat, I need to plod on. I have a PM I need to perform."

"Good luck. Speak later."

Des hung up on her, but Sam wasn't narked by his rudeness. She was used to it by now and had learnt to accept it was who he was and how he treated everyone, not just her. She returned to the interview room to find it silent. "Forgive me for being so long."

"This is totally unacceptable to keep my client waiting like this, Inspector," Davidson admonished her.

"It was out of my hands, I'm afraid." She retook her seat and nodded for Bob to restart the recording. "Ah, yes. I've received confirmation that Miss Mitchell left the hotel the following morning and that she stayed in the room next to Jason Flintoff's. Did it have a connecting door?"

"No, it did not. Can I go now?"

"Not yet. There are a few more questions I'd like to ask you before you leave."

"Well, get on with it."

"We're going to need to take a sample of your DNA."

"What? Why? She can't do this, can she?" Vanessa shouted at Davidson.

"We'll give her what she wants, just to keep the peace. Otherwise, she might see it as obstructing a police investigation."

"I'll get a test now." Sam bolted out of the room again. "Nick, the officer hasn't left for the lab yet, have they?"

"Not yet. Why?"

"Give me another test. I might as well have Vanessa Mitchell's DNA to hand, just in case."

"Makes sense." He produced another kit from under the counter and handed it to her.

"Did Warren get off all right?"

"Yes. He did the test and left immediately. What a mess this case is for you. I don't envy you one iota, ma'am."

"Thanks, Nick. I'm determined to get to the bottom of this."

"I have every confidence in you. Let me know if I can lend a hand."

"I will. Thanks. And I haven't forgotten about you joining our team either. The DCI appears to be dragging his heels on that one. I'll remind him how urgent it is to fill Alex's shoes."

"No rush, ma'am. I'm grateful for the opportunity to work with your team."

"Remind me to chase it up later." She walked back down the corridor, her legs aching from all the running around she'd had to do already that day.

She took the DNA sample from Vanessa and then set her free.

"What? Is that it?"

"Yes, all of this could have been avoided if Miss Mitchell hadn't kicked up a fuss in her office. I'm satisfied that her alibi has checked out."

"What a load of nonsense and wasted time this experience has been today. You made a show of me in front of my colleagues. I won't forget that, Inspector."

Sam cocked an eyebrow. "Another threat, Miss Mitchell? We had every right to question you, as you are considered a significant person of interest in this investigation."

"You're kidding me? You still think I started the fire?" Vanessa spat at her. "I've already told you I was nowhere near it, and my alibi backs that up."

"We'll see. Further checks will be carried out. Someone started that fire, and you had a genuine motive to kill Helen after sleeping with her husband. You might have paid someone to do it and used your trip to Carlisle as the perfect excuse to not be around."

"That's utter bullshit. Grasping at straws again, that's all that is."

Sam smiled and showed Vanessa and her solicitor back to the reception area.

"Will you give me a lift back to the office?" Vanessa asked Davidson.

"Yes, if I have to."

"I'd rather that than get a lift back in a police car," she snapped back at him.

They left the building without saying anything further, which was a relief to Sam. She and Bob climbed the stairs to the incident room.

"What kept you?" Bob asked.

"I'll tell you in a moment."

He grunted his disapproval. When they reached the office, he made them all a drink.

"Any news from the boys yet, Claire?"

"Oliver checked in with me about ten minutes ago. No sign of any footage being available. All the neighbours are elderly around there."

Sam rested her backside on a nearby desk. "That's a shame. What that poor woman went through and not to have any evidence as to who did it to her... well, it's not helpful, is it? On top of losing her sister in a devastating fire, it would be remiss of us not to connect the two crimes."

Bob handed around the coffees. "We've got to link them. Has someone got it in for the family? Has something happened in their past, maybe before Jason came on the scene?"

Sam sipped at her coffee and sighed. "Hard to know at this stage. Yet another angle we need to look at. I'd like to run a full background check on Vanessa Mitchell. Can I leave that with you, Claire?"

"I should be able to squeeze it in this afternoon, boss."

"Right, are you going to tell us why you were absent from the interview for so long?"

"Sorry, yes. I chased up Vanessa's alibi with the manager of the hotel. I made the call from my office. When I ended the call, I happened to glance out of the window, and I spotted Warren Goldman standing by his vehicle in the car park. I raced down there to ask him what he was up to."

"What the heck?" Bob said, mortified. He sank into his chair. "What did he have to say for himself?"

"He must have been following us, wanted to know why we'd brought Vanessa in and what she'd said. I told him to back off and leave the investigation to us."

"Was he satisfied with that?"

"I think so. He appeared to be more concerned about the baby Helen was carrying."

"Shit! Does he think it's his?" Bob asked. He twisted his mug on the desk.

"Yes. I've told him we'll do a DNA test."

"I can't believe this is happening."

"Simmer down, partner. He has a right to know, especially after telling me that Jason is infertile."

Bob smacked his hands over his face. "I didn't know. What a bloody mess!"

"Have you spoken to him lately?"

"No, I thought I'd take a step back and allow him to grieve. Do you want me to check in with him?"

"It might be an idea. Vanessa said she hadn't heard from him, either."

"Bugger. I hope he's okay. There's something more to this investigation, isn't there? What with Davina being held hostage as well."

"You're not wrong. Go on, give him a call now. If nothing else, it'll put our minds at rest."

Bob withdrew his phone from his pocket and asked, "Is that why you requested the DNA sample from Vanessa?"

"I just thought I'd kill two birds with one stone. I doubt if anything will show up. Better to be safe than sorry, and she was giving us that much grief, I thought it would slap her down a bit."

Bob sniggered. "It did that all right. It's ringing..." He shook his head. "Nope, he's not picking up, it's gone straight to voicemail. I'm worried about him now. Where can he be?"

"Could he be staying with another friend? Might be worth calling all the hotels in the area, see if he's registered with any of them."

"I'll do it now."

Sam's mobile rang. She looked at the caller ID and saw Crystal's name listed. "It's my sister. I'll take it in the office." She took her mug with her and answered the call en route. "Hey, sis. How are you?"

"Still devastated by the news, but that's not why I'm ringing you."

"You sound stressed. Take a breath and tell me what's wrong."

"I had a feeling something like this was going to happen."

"Like what? You're not making any sense. Are you sitting down yet?"

"Yes, I'm at my desk and I've shut the shop."

"Why? Are you feeling all right? You're not ill, are you?"

"No. Oh, Sam. What have we done?"

"Wait, as far as I know, we haven't done anything wrong. What are you getting at? Come on, love, the suspense is killing me. Oh God, it's not Dad, is it?"

"No. It's Mike."

"Crap. What's he done now?"

"He's in hospital. Fighting for his life."

7

Sam didn't wait to hear what else her sister had to say. "I'm coming to get you. I'll be there in ten minutes." She drove like a maniac through Workington to the boutique.

Crystal was outside the shop, waiting for her.

"Tell me what happened."

"I got the shock of my life when the prison rang me. It was news to me that Mike had listed me as his next of kin."

"I didn't know either. I suppose it makes sense. You've always been closer to him than anyone else, including Mum and Dad."

"You're probably right."

"What did the prison say?"

"He was in a fight with a group of prisoners over the usual thing: drugs."

"He will never learn. How bad is he?"

"He's got life-threatening injuries, that's all they would tell me."

Sam sighed and pushed her foot down on the accelerator to squeeze past the lights before they changed. "My stomach is in knots. It's been years since we've seen him. I'm not sure how he's going to react to me showing up with you."

"I couldn't have come alone. I'm glad you suggested coming with me. Thanks, sis."

Sam reached for her sister's hand. "I'm always with you, you know that."

"I know. The guilt is seeping in, though. It's always been you and me against the world. I guess Mike has had his nose pushed out of joint on more than one occasion, which led him to turn to drugs, didn't it?"

"Sadly true. But that says more about him than us, Crystal. You have nothing to feel guilty about, and neither do I. It's all about the choices that we make in life."

SAM DREW into the hospital car park and placed her notice on the dashboard. Then, she and Crystal ran up the slight hill to the A and E Department. Sam flashed her ID at the male receptionist and lowered her voice to tell him why they were there.

"Ah, yes. I know who you're talking about. Let me check with the doctor to find out if you're free to see him. I won't be long."

Sam and Crystal spent the next five minutes on tenterhooks in the waiting area, which was full to the brim.

"Spot the sick person? Can you see anyone bleeding out, whose leg is dangling at an awkward angle?" Crystal complained.

"Blimey, I thought you had morphed into Bob then. That's the type of thing he would say. A and E ain't what it used to be, is it?"

"So true. I've heard there's a shortage of doctors in the area. Patients can't get into their surgeries, so they descend on this place by the dozen. It's a shambolic situation, that's what it is. My friend came here a couple of weeks ago. She had a seven-hour wait before she saw a doctor."

"That's scary. I hope she was all right?"

"Not really. She was admitted and had her appendix removed."

"Ouch. She must have been doubled over with pain, and yet she still had to wait that long to be seen. Makes you wonder in what direction the NHS is heading. Hopefully, the new government will stop the rot."

Crystal tutted. "You reckon? I know they gave the doctors and nurses a pay rise as soon as they came into power, but I have my doubts if that will appease the staff for long. Anyway, it was the junior doctors who received the pay rise. I think the nurses rejected theirs, but I could be wrong."

"We'll have to see how it pans out in the next few years. I suppose we need to give them a fair crack of the whip after being on the sidelines for the past fourteen years."

"If you say so. It was unforgivable to strip most of the pensioners of their Winter Fuel Payment."

"I was right. You have turned into Bob."

They both laughed.

"I hope the receptionist isn't going to be too much longer," Sam said. "How are you feeling?"

"Nervous, apprehensive, and a little curious at the same time. I wonder if he's going to pull through."

"We'll have to wait and see. Do you think it's wrong of us not to let Dad know?"

Crystal sighed. "I reckon it's going to be a case of damned if we do and damned if we don't."

"I thought that, too. We'll have to gauge it once we lay eyes on him. I can't say I'm looking forward to it, but at the end of the day, he's family, and we're all he's got."

Sam peered over her shoulder when the door whooshed open behind her.

The receptionist smiled and said, "Please, come with me. Sorry about the delay. The doctor was still examining him."

"Can you tell us how he is?"

"I'd rather you spoke to the doctor about his condition. It's not for me to say."

They walked side by side through the wide corridor until it narrowed at the end.

"Take a seat. I'll pop my head in and let the doctor know you're here."

"Thank you."

Crystal sat in one of the chairs outside the room, but Sam chose to stand. It wasn't long before she started pacing the area.

"Do you always do that when you're nervous? I've never noticed in the past."

"Sorry, it's a habit. I frequently drive Bob nuts. I'll sit down."

The receptionist reappeared with a female doctor close behind him. "This is Doctor Lincoln. I'll leave you to it and get back to work."

"Thank you for looking after us," Sam said.

He smiled and rushed back through the corridor to his station.

"How is he, Doctor?" Sam got to her feet and asked.

"Please, sit down. The news isn't good, I'm afraid. Your brother has been stabbed multiple times. We're going to need to operate. We're waiting for the surgeon to arrive."

"What sort of operation?"

"One that will hopefully save his life. The CT scan we carried out when he arrived revealed that his lung was ruptured and there is significant internal bleeding. His liver was also damaged in the attack."

Sam closed her eyes and shook her head. "What are his chances?"

"Slim, very slim at best. But we're going to do our very best to save him, hence flying in a doctor from Newcastle, rather than sending your brother over there."

"Thank you, we appreciate it. Can we see him?"

"For a few moments. We haven't had a chance to clean him up yet. So you'll need to be prepared for the worst."

"I'm a serving police officer. I've been confronted with serious injuries before, although this will be my sister's first time. Unless you want to stay here, Crystal, and leave this to me?"

"No way. Stop protecting me. I'm prepared. It's me the prison contacted as his next of kin. I should see him, no matter what state he's in."

Sam flung an arm around her sister's shoulder and kissed her on the cheek. Then she told the doctor, "We're ready."

The doctor opened the door and led them into a room large enough for a hospital bed, with a few feet to spare on either side. Sam guided her sister around the other side of the bed and clung to her tightly. She stared at her battered and bruised brother, and the hand of fate squeezed her heart.

"Oh God. He looks awful."

Crystal sobbed beside her and reached out to touch Mike's cheek with a shaking hand. "Oh, Mike, will you ever be able to forgive us?"

At the sound of her voice, his eyes flickered open, although he didn't smile at either of them. "Sis, you made it. Thanks for coming." His gaze rested on Crystal.

"How do you feel, Mike?" Sam asked the most obvious question she could summon.

"Like a demolition ball has struck me. How do you think I frigging feel?"

He coughed violently, and the doctor had to step in to calm him down.

"Okay, and breathe slowly but deeply. Try not to speak. Are you comfortable with both your sisters being here with you?"

The coughing died down enough for him to mutter, "Yes, let them both stay."

The doctor held the stethoscope to his chest and encouraged him to breathe in and out a few more times, the way she had advised him to. "That's better. Please take things easy. You shouldn't overexert yourself."

"What's wrong with me? Can you fix whatever is wrong? Or is this it? Am I on my way out?"

"We're going to do our best for you. The surgeon is on his way. The second he's here, we'll whisk you off to surgery and see how things are inside."

"What? You're going to operate?" His breathing worsened, and the doctor slipped an oxygen mask over his nose and mouth.

"Hush now, Mike. Listen to the doctor. It's okay, we'll be here when you wake up," Sam reassured him.

His gaze fell on her, and for the first time in years, she spotted a snippet of love showing in his eyes, which caught her off guard for a fleeting moment before it disappeared again.

"Still banging people like me up for a living, are you, sis?"

"I arrest people who have committed serious crimes and put them through the system, yes."

"I thought as much. You still come across as a mean-spirited bitch."

The bitterness in his tone shouldn't have shocked her, but it did. "I'll wait outside so you can talk to Crystal by yourself. Wishing you well, brother."

"Don't insult my intelligence, you two-faced bitch. You'd like nothing more than to see the back of me. Go on, admit it?" He coughed again.

"I'm sorry. I can't allow this conversation to continue," the doctor said. "I'm going to have to ask you both to leave the room."

"No. I want Crystal to stay," Mike spluttered, his breath coming in short, sharp bursts.

"It's fine by me. I'll be outside, Crystal. Take as long as you need. I'm not in a rush to get back." Her gaze flitted between her siblings once more.

Crystal's eyes pleaded with her to stay, but Sam shook her head and left the room without saying anything else to her brother.

She sank into the chair outside and buried her head in her hands. Unexpected tears trickled through her fingers. She withdrew a tissue from a packet she kept in her pocket and blew her nose. Removing another one, she dried her eyes, determined not to let her sister see the state she was in when she eventually joined her.

A nurse walked past. "Are you okay?" she stopped to ask.

"I'm fine. Just a little overwhelmed. Thanks for asking, though."

"Of course. Would you like me to get you a drink?"

"No, I'll be okay in a moment."

The nurse smiled and went on her way, leaving Sam to contemplate what to do next. Her emotional sister joined her a few minutes later and sat beside her. "Are you all right?"

"I will be. I'm sorry he was tough on you in there. I'm sure deep down he didn't mean it. I think he was putting on a front, masking his true feelings."

"Possibly. I thought I saw a change in his eyes at one point, but it didn't last long. My being there was only making matters worse. That's why I decided to leave. How is he?"

"Resting, the visiting left him exhausted. I'm riddled with guilt, Sam. I truly didn't expect to have any feelings for him after all this time. I was wrong. He's still our brother, no matter what crimes he's committed in the past."

Sam clutched her hand as a porter arrived and knocked on the door. "The surgeon must be here."

The doctor came to see them. She confirmed that Sam's instincts were correct.

"Don't worry, we'll take good care of him."

"How long will the operation take, Doctor?" Sam asked.

"Between two and three hours. It depends on how bad the internal bleeding is when the surgeon gets in there. Will you be sticking around?"

"I can stay here if you need to get back, Sam," her sister said.

"No, I'll stay with you. I'll need to contact the team to let them know what the state of play is."

"I'll leave you to it. There's a family room down the corridor if you'd prefer to relocate. You'll be more comfortable in there. I'll let you know how your brother is the second I know. I want to assure you that he's in the best hands possible. Mr Randall is a renowned surgeon in his field."

"Thank you, Doctor. We'll keep our fingers crossed that everything goes well for Mike."

The doctor sped up the corridor to catch up with the porter. She ran ahead of him to open the door in front of them, and then they were gone.

Crystal had a meltdown beside her.

"Come on, let's get settled in the family room. We'll have more privacy in there, sweetheart."

Crystal wiped her tears on the sleeve of her padded jacket. They linked arms and walked off.

"Here it is. I'll just bring my team up to date and then I'll go in search of a coffee."

"No, you do what you have to do. I'll fetch the drinks. Coffee with one?"

"You're a star, thanks, Crystal." Sam withdrew a handful of silver she kept in her pocket and handed it to her sister.

"That's what I love about you the most. You're always prepared for every eventuality."

"I try to be. Mum used to be the same, didn't she?"

"She did. Oh God, I miss her so much. She'd know what to do for the best, wouldn't she?"

"That she would. We'll figure it out over a cup of coffee."

"In other words, get a move on."

Sam grinned, and Crystal set off in search of the nearest vending machine. She inhaled and exhaled several times and then made her first call. She rang Bob's mobile. He answered after the first ring.

"How are things? We've been waiting to hear from you."

"My brother is in a bad way. They've just taken him down for surgery. I've decided to wait here with Crystal."

"Yes, I don't blame you. Was he awake?"

"He was. I witnessed glimpses of the brother he used to be, but only for a moment. His anger soon returned, and I left the room rather than get him worked up. How are things going there?"

"Not good. I've tried leaving Jason messages. I've called every hotel in the area, and not one of them has him listed. I've even called his office. They haven't seen him all week, and they didn't know about the fire."

"What the fuck? Why wouldn't he have informed them?"

"My thoughts exactly. I'm at a loss about what to do for the best, Sam. I'm worried about him. It's not like him to disappear like this."

"Shit. Try not to think the worst, mate. Can you go through his SM accounts and contact some of his friends?"

"Good call. I'll get on it now."

"Are Oliver and Liam still out?"

"Yes. I rang them a while back. They're finishing up there and coming back to base. They sounded frustrated."

"They're not the only ones, are they? It looks like I'm going to be stuck here for a few hours. I'll stay with Crystal for a while, and if it's all right with my sister, I'll nip upstairs and check how Davina is getting on."

"There you go again, always thinking about this place when you have personal stuff you need to deal with. Have you told your dad?"

"No, we've debated calling him. We're not sure whether to involve him. Maybe we'll reassess that while Mike's having the surgery."

"Personally, if it were my kid in there, no matter what he'd done in the past, I'd want to know. But thankfully, I'm not the one who has to make the choice. You are."

"Thanks, partner. Trust you to make me feel guiltier than I already am."

"I... didn't mean to do that," he stuttered, to her amusement.

"I'm teasing you. Call me if you locate Jason. It's funny that he hasn't contacted anyone, not even his bit on the side. Vanessa said she hadn't seen him since he checked out of the hotel either, so there's no point calling her."

"Unless she's lying."

"Hmm... now there's a thought. Maybe you should divert the boys. We could put Vanessa under surveillance. It might also be worth putting an alert out for Jason's car. Have a word with Nick."

"On it now. Take care, Sam. Check in with us when you can. We'll hold your brother in our thoughts for now."

"Bless you. I'm going before my emotional side takes over."

He laughed and ended the call.

Sam crossed the room to the noticeboard and read that until Crystal returned with the drinks.

"That was quite a trek. They should have more vending machines in this place."

"There's a café near the main entrance. I guess most visitors tend to go there."

"That's on the other side of the building now. Never mind. How are things back at the station?"

"Bob's as frustrated as ever. His mate, Helen's husband, has gone missing. He's doing everything he can to find him."

"Would he be with his parents?"

"I've left Bob going through his social media accounts. He'll find him sooner or later. I have a favour to ask." Sam pointed at the comfy seats behind them, and they both sat.

"What do you need, Sam?"

"I wondered if it would be all right if I left you and checked on Davina while I was here."

Crystal tutted and waved her free hand. "Of course. You daft mare, you don't have to ask my permission. It makes sense for you to visit her, rather than sit around with boring old me, twiddling our thumbs."

"Nonsense, I'd much rather sit here with you, but I feel compelled to see how she's doing and if she's regained her sight yet."

"Honestly, it doesn't matter to me. Hey, we have a more important matter to discuss before you go."

"Whether to tell Dad?"

Crystal sighed. "I was thinking about it on my way to get the drinks."

"And what was the conclusion?"

"I think we should call him. I think he'd be furious, maybe even hurt, if he found out. We have to consider the downside of him having the operation. What if he doesn't pull through?"

"I ran it past Bob, and he said pretty much the same thing. Do you want to call him, or should I do it?"

"You're braver than me."

Sam snorted. "Not all the time. You were far braver than me when we were kids."

"And Mike was braver than both of us put together."

"So true. Go on, you can wind him around your little finger."

Crystal rolled her eyes and withdrew her mobile from her jacket pocket. She placed her cup on the floor and grasped Sam's hand as she made the call. "I'll put it on speaker. It'll save me having to repeat what he says."

Sam nodded and crossed her fingers. "You've got this."

"Hello, Crystal. How are you?" Their father said. "I'm just on my way out to the supermarket. Can I give you a call later when I get back?"

"Umm... I'd rather talk now, Dad, if that's all right."

"I suppose my shopping expedition can wait. I've found this is the perfect time to go before the mums pick the kids up from school."

"Dad, I've got some news I need to share with you. You might want to take a seat first."

"Lordy, now you're worrying me. Is everything all right? Has something happened to either you or your sister?"

"No. Sam's here with me now."

"Hi, Dad."

"Sam? Please, will you just tell me what's going on? You're scaring the crap out of me, girls."

"Okay. It's not easy to say this, so please don't interrupt."

"I wouldn't. Tell me."

"It's Mike."

Their father groaned.

"Hear me out, Dad. You said you wouldn't interrupt."

"I'm listening. What's he done now?"

"About an hour ago, I received a call from the prison."

Their father gasped.

"He's been injured in an attack. Sam and I are at Whitehaven Hospital now. Mike's in surgery."

"Jesus. Is he all right?"

"He's seriously injured; a few of his major organs were damaged in the attack. It's touch and go whether he makes it. We weren't sure if you'd want to know or not."

"I'll be right there. Of course I'd want to know. He's still my son. I know he refused to come to your mother's funeral, but..."

"That's a relief. He's going to be in the theatre for at least two hours."

"All right. I'll come straight away. You've done the right thing, ringing me. Maybe it's time we put the past behind us and thought about the future."

"We'll see you soon, Dad. Drive carefully."

"I always do. I might stop off at the supermarket on the way."

"Come to A and E when you get here. Give me a call, and either Sam or I will come and get you."

"I'll see you both soon. I love you both very much."

"We love you, too, Dad," they said in unison.

Crystal ended the call and then hugged Sam, the relief clear in both of them.

After a warm embrace, Crystal pushed away from Sam. "You go and see Davina. Hopefully, you'll be back before Dad gets here."

"If you're sure?"

"Go. I'll bore myself silly in your absence, looking through one of the magazines."

"Shame there isn't a bridal mag amongst them."

"I have them coming out of my ears back at the boutique."

Sam kissed her sister again and left the room. She walked to the end of the corridor and hopped on the lift, which took her to the third floor where Davina was admitted. She showed her ID to the nurse sitting at the desk as she entered the ward.

"Oh, okay. And who are you here to see?"

"Davina Baldwin. How is she?"

The nurse picked up a clipboard on her right and ran her finger down the list of patients. "Sorry, I've only just come on duty. Well, that's strange."

"What is?" Sam asked, not liking the nurse's tone.

"She discharged herself earlier today, around lunchtime. Let me check with a colleague, see if I can get any further information for you."

"She what? What about her eyesight? Has it returned?"

"That's all I can tell you. I won't be long."

Sam was left feeling shocked until the nurse came back. "Well? What can you tell me?"

"Her parents left before lunch. As soon as they left, Davina asked for a sandwich and a drink. When my colleague checked if she wanted anything else, she found Davina getting dressed."

"And her eyesight?"

"She said it was a miracle and that she could see again."

Sam shook her head, finding it hard to believe. "This is incredible. Have you ever heard of this happening before?"

"Not me personally. I dare say it happens occasionally, especially after someone has received a bang to the head. Marie told me that she seemed chirpy enough when she left."

"Maybe it was the relief of regaining her sight."

"More than likely. Is there anything else I can do for you?"

"No. I'm dealing with a personal issue at the hospital at the moment. I'll drop by Davina's house and check how she is on the way home."

"That's kind of you. All in the line of duty, eh?"

"You could say that. Thanks for your help." Her mind swirled like it was in the eye of a tornado as she made her way back to Crystal. Gathering her thoughts together, she called Bob.

"Hi, has something happened to your brother?"

"No. It's not that. I thought I'd check how Davina was doing instead of sitting around waiting for news."

"And? How's she doing?"

"You're never going to believe this. She's not here."

"Shit! You're not telling me that she's been abducted from her hospital bed, are you? Because that would have to be a first."

"No. Quite the opposite. She discharged herself not long after they gave her lunch."

"Discharged herself? But they were keeping her in for observation. What about her eyesight? I can't get my head around this."

"You're not the only one. From what I can gather, her eyesight returned, and she was desperate to get out of here."

"That's not right. Why did they let her go? Wouldn't she have a concussion after being struck so hard—hard enough to temporarily blind her?"

"Both valid questions that I'm having trouble answering. Hang on, if this all happened a couple of hours ago, wouldn't the boys have said they'd seen her at the house?"

"You tell me. Want me to give them a call?"

"No. I'll do it. Keep trying to find Jason. Something isn't adding up to me, and whatever is going on, I'm determined to get to the bottom of it."

"Believe me, I'm trying."

Sam jabbed the END button and immediately dialled Oliver's number. "Hi, it's me. Are you still at Davina's house?"

"Actually, we were about to leave, boss. SOCO is still here. They're asking if we can secure the front door that Bob broke down."

"Get onto Nick at the station and ask him to arrange for someone to repair the door. Has Davina shown up?"

"Er, no. I thought she was in hospital," Oliver queried.

"She was. She discharged herself. I thought she might head home."

"Do you want us to hang around here, just in case she shows up?"

"Yes, someone should be there until her property is deemed safe again. I'll leave that with you. Call me if Davina shows up."

"Got it, boss."

Sam upped her pace once more and opened the door to the family room to find their father hugging her sister. They both turned to face her, and she rushed to join them in a group hug.

"Hi, Dad. I'm glad to see you here."

"You look exhausted. Have you been taking care of yourself properly?" their father asked.

"I was about to ask you the same. You've lost weight. Have you been eating?"

"I pick mostly. I have to admit, I haven't had a decent meal since your mother passed away."

Sam took a step back and shook her head. "You should have told us. You know you're welcome at our place."

"And mine," Crystal chipped in.

"I know." He moved away from them and sat in a comfy chair. "I've got to cope, though. I refuse to be a burden to you two."

"You could never be a burden, Dad. We love you. We're worried about you."

He smiled. "There's no need. I'm getting by the best I can. Enough about me. What about Mike? Are you going to tell me what happened to him?"

Sam glanced at Crystal, and her sister relayed the information she'd received from the prison which had brought them here.

"Drugs—it's always about the drugs, isn't it?" Their father shook his head in disgust. "How in God's name does it get inside in the first place? These men aren't punished when they go to prison, far from it."

"They are, Dad," Sam replied. "But there's a lack of staff in prisons these days. They need to have their eyes and ears everywhere. It's a well-known fact that gangs are always searching for ways to get the drugs inside."

"I understand. It still shouldn't be allowed. What did the doctor say about his injuries?"

"They're life-threatening, that's why they've taken him down for surgery. I think it's the internal bleeding they're more concerned about."

"How has it come to this? Mike was such a good boy growing up; we never had any problems with him. Not until he branched out on his own. I told his mother it was too soon, but he was adamant to leave us when he was eighteen, with no prospects as an apprentice steelworker. What type of job is that for a quiet lad like him? Once he got in with the wrong crowd, he became disrespectful towards your mother, which caused a rift between us. All of it could have been avoided if only he hadn't left home when he did."

"There's no point in us living in the past, Dad," Sam said. "It's the future we need to be concerned about. He's reached out to Crystal for a reason."

"Probably to tap her up for money to buy more drugs on the inside," their father snapped and folded his arms.

"We'll have to wait and see what he has to say if he makes it through the operation."

"Did you speak with him before he was taken away?"

"Crystal did. I tried to no avail, there was still an underlying conflict between us. Rather than cause problems, I left the room."

"He always hated you becoming a copper."

Sam shrugged. "That's tough. It's not like I chose the career just to piss him off. I happen to be good at it. He needs to accept that or we're back to square one. I won't be able to move forward if he wants a relationship with me in the future. Which I doubt will be the case, anyway, so I'm not sure why we're sitting here discussing it."

"Don't say that, Sam. He's up for parole soon, maybe that's why he was attacked, out of jealousy," Crystal suggested.

"And what happens when he comes out? Will he have an eye on one of us putting him up? Sorry, you can count me out."

"And me," their father chipped in.

Crystal groaned and left her seat. "How can you both sit there and say that, knowing that he might not make it through the operation?"

"It's hard to forgive and forget, love. It's going to take time to regain our trust," their father said.

Crystal turned away from them, and Sam could tell her sister was struggling to hold back the tears. She left her seat and tried to comfort Crystal, but she shrugged her arm off.

"I won't be able to live with the guilt... if he dies. We all turned our backs on him. He didn't deserve to be treated like this. We're at fault, not him."

"Good Lord, your mother would be turning in her grave if she heard you say that, Crystal."

Crystal spun around to face their father. "Would she? I don't think she would, Dad. Don't you understand? There's a chance we could lose him."

Their father sighed heavily, placed his elbows on his thighs and rested his chin on his clenched fists. "Because of the choices he made in this life. This has nothing to do with the way he treated his family, although that still sticks in my throat. You weren't there that day…"

Sam crossed the room and sat next to their father. She looped an arm around his shoulder. "Dad? What day are you talking about?"

"I've said too much. I swore to your mother that I would never tell you."

"You can't tell us that. If he did something wrong, we have a right to know."

Their father remained silent, and a cloud of confusion descended.

"Dad," Sam urged. She was determined to get to the truth of why their family had split apart all those years ago.

"All right. I need to get it out. Maybe then I will start to heal. They say the truth will set us free, don't they?"

Sam nodded. "That's true, Dad. What did Mike do?"

"I came home from work; he was nineteen at the time. I stepped through the front door to hear Mike and your mother arguing in the kitchen. I entered the room to see what the hell was going on. I found your mother pinned to the wall by your brother."

"What? That's terrible," Sam was the first to say.

"Yes, how awful. I'm sorry that happened, Dad," Crystal added.

Their father reached for both of their hands. He squeezed them tightly and told them the rest of the story. "That's not all; he was holding a knife to her throat. I found myself frozen to the spot. Caught up in a dilemma. If I pounced on him, he might have ended your mother's life there and then. I decided to try to talk him down. It worked, but at a cost."

"What cost?" Sam asked, fearful of what their father was about to reveal.

"He told us that he would leave us alone if we handed over twenty thousand. If we refused, he would slit your mother's throat." Their father broke out in a sweat. "Shit, look at the state of me. What in God's name am I doing here? I shouldn't be here, not after what he put me and your mother through."

"You paid him?" Crystal asked.

"I had to, otherwise he would have killed your mother."

"Oh, Dad. I'm so sorry you and Mum were subjected to such a dreadful ordeal. No wonder you both turned your backs on him."

"We did it to protect the two of you," he muttered and squeezed their hands tighter.

"I don't understand," Sam said. "What do you mean?"

Their father gulped. "He told us that he would kill your mother and then come after you. Both of you."

Sam stared at Crystal as the news sank in.

"Jesus," Sam said. "So you paid him the twenty grand."

"Which led him down a slippery road of buying yet more drugs," Crystal added.

"That's right. What would you have done in my situation?" he asked, turning to each of them.

Sam released her hand from his and hugged him tightly. "I would have done the same. Dad, you have nothing to feel guilty about. He's at fault, not you, not us. Mike is his own worst enemy. I'm glad you finally told us. I'm sorry. I want nothing more to do with him." She rose from her seat.

Crystal gasped and stood to confront her. "What? You can't walk away now; I won't let you. If he dies, the guilt will eat away at you for the rest of your life."

"It won't, sis. Because I refuse to allow it to. This ends today. Mike chose to live a life on drugs. Did you hear what Dad just said? He held a knife to our mother's throat."

"I heard. He was desperate."

Sam paced the floor and glared at her sister. "Stop making excuses for him. Would you still be saying the same if he'd followed through with his threat? Killed our mother and then came after us?"

"Now you're being ridiculous," Crystal shouted.

"Stop it! Now I wish I had kept my mouth shut." Their father buried his head in his hands and sobbed.

Sam was shocked. She'd only ever seen their father break down and cry like this once before: the night their mother had died. She rushed to sit beside him. "We're sorry, Dad. He's doing it again; even though he's not in the room with us, he's tearing us apart."

Their father shrugged her arm off. "I'm okay. I should never have told you. Your mother and I have hidden this secret from you both for years. I'm weak. I buckled at the first sign of trouble. I'm nothing without your mother beside me."

"Don't say that, Dad. It simply isn't true," Sam pleaded, tears pricking her eyes.

The door opened, and the doctor entered the room. "Hello, I've got news for you all. It was touch and go there for a moment or two. We lost Mike as he had a problem with his heart, but we managed to bring him back. He will take time to heal, but there is no reason why he shouldn't make a full recovery."

"That's fantastic news, thank you, Doctor," Crystal gushed.

Sam and their father stared at each other. She knew there would be a long road of mistrust and judgement ahead of them, and so did their father.

"I'll leave you to it," the doctor said and exited the room.

"Well, I'm pleased he's going to make it, aren't you?" Crystal asked.

"I can't do this any more," Sam said. "I love you both too much. I'm going to leave now. Glad he's going to be all right. However, it doesn't change the way I feel about him. If anything, what Dad told us has only made things much clearer for me. I have an important investigation I need to get back to. Dad, will you give Crystal a ride home?"

"Yes, you go, love. Give me a call tonight when you get the chance."

She hugged them both. Crystal's hug was lacklustre, to say the least—understandable in the circumstances.

Sam tore through the corridors and back to her car. She sat for a few moments before her heart returned to its regular beat. She felt like she had wasted two hours of her life she wouldn't get back. Her brother had succeeded in putting a wedge between them; it's what he did best.

8

"You're back. How's your brother?" Bob asked as soon as she set foot in the incident room.

"I'd rather not discuss it. I'm in dire need of caffeine, partner, if you wouldn't mind."

To oblige, Bob left his seat, and she went through to her office. He found her staring out of the window at the hills beyond.

"Now you're worrying me. You only stand there when you have the weight of the world on your shoulders. Did your brother die?"

She kept facing the window, unable to trust herself not to break down. "No. He made it through. Grab yourself a coffee and join me."

"I'll be right back."

By the time he returned, Sam had summoned up enough strength to make it to her chair and gather her wits about her.

"Well?" Bob asked.

"He made it. But is it wrong of me to stand here and wish he hadn't?"

"What the...? This isn't like you, Sam. What's going on?"

Needing to unburden herself, she told him what their father had revealed at the hospital.

"Jesus. That's insane. No wonder your parents distanced themselves from him. Who could blame them?"

"I don't. I never have. But I didn't know this was the reason why they didn't want to have anything else to do with him. I'm shocked and appalled."

"What did Crystal say?"

"She was shocked, too. She's insisting she's going to stick by Mike to help him get over the operation."

"And you've fallen out with her over her decision?"

"Sort of. I'm not sure how I feel about it. I made my excuses and left. Told them I was in the middle of an important investigation."

"Which is true. Talking of which, I still can't get hold of Jason. I've rung several mutual friends, but he hasn't been in touch with anyone. Now I'm seriously worried about him."

"What about his parents? Have you tried them?"

"I did. They're on holiday in Spain. They've been there for the past four months at their holiday home."

"Does he have a key to their house in the UK?"

Bob cringed and thumped his thigh. "I forgot to ask. I'll call them back."

"Make sure you ask for their address as well."

He raised his eyebrows. "I know where they live."

"Don't bother disturbing them a second time, then. We'll nip round there and see for ourselves if it's not too far."

"It's not. It's about ten minutes away."

"What about Oliver and Liam? Have they reported back yet? I rang them to make them aware of the situation with Davina."

"Not heard from them since."

Sam placed her hands on either side of her temples. "Why the fuck would Davina put herself in danger again, like this?"

"Maybe she knows more than she's letting on?"

Sam tilted her head. "Such as?"

He shrugged. "I don't know, it seemed a good idea to say it. Don't forget someone held her hostage."

"I haven't, far from it. So, the wife dies, the husband goes missing after showing up at the devastated house, and the victim's sister is held hostage and then banged over the head with a heavy object, hospitalising her."

"Only because we showed up at her door. She might have died if we hadn't."

"That's true. God, we're no further forward, are we? I'm going to call the Baldwins. Ask them if they have any idea why Davina discharged herself." Sam took a sip from her mug.

"I'll get back to it. Give you some space."

"Thanks, Bob."

He closed the door behind him, and Sam made the call.

"Mr Baldwin. Hi, it's Sam Cobbs. Is Davina with you?"

"What? Are you crazy? She's in hospital, or had you forgotten that, Inspector?"

"No, I hadn't forgotten. I've just been to the hospital on personal business. While I was there, I thought I'd drop by to see how your daughter was getting on. Imagine my surprise when the nurse told me that she discharged herself after eating lunch today."

"What? This is news to me."

"What's going on?" Linda Baldwin asked in the background.

"It's Davina. No, she's not on the phone. I'm speaking with the inspector. She's informed me that Davina has discharged herself."

"She can't have. She's blind. Are you sure?" Linda asked. "Give me the phone. Let me talk to her... Inspector? What's all this nonsense you've been telling my husband?"

"Hello, Linda. I'm sorry, it's true. I was at the hospital visiting a relative and thought I would check how Davina was doing. The nurse told me that she left after she ate her lunch."

"I... I don't want to say. I can't work that child out. And you thought she had come home with us?"

"That's what I was hoping. The nurse told me that you'd already left the hospital, though. Oh, no..."

"What? Have you thought of something?"

"I didn't ask the nurse if she'd left alone. What she did tell me was that Davina had miraculously regained her sight and could see again."

"She has? Why hasn't she contacted us to stop us from worrying?"

"I don't know. If she's not with you, do you have any idea where she's likely to be?"

"At home, I suppose. But your guess is as good as mine. I clearly have no idea what is going on in that woman's mind."

"She's not at home. SOCO and two members of my team are still in the vicinity."

Linda started crying, and her husband took over the conversation again.

"We don't know what's going on, Inspector. I wish we knew, but that child has always been a law unto herself. She's driven us both insane over the years with her deplorable antics."

"Okay. Thanks for speaking to me. I'll see what we can do to try and find her. Please try not to worry."

"Easier said than done. What an insensitive so-and-so she is. How can she do this after the week we've had? Selfish to the core, she is, always has been, and I can't see her altering her ways anytime soon."

"I'll speak to you soon, Mr Baldwin. Take care of each other."

Sam ended the call and threw her phone on the desk. She scratched her head, unsure how to proceed. Exasperated, she joined Bob and Claire in the outer office. "Here's some news for you: the Baldwins haven't seen or heard from Davina. They were gobsmacked when I told them she'd left the hospital. I'm wondering if someone was there, waiting for her."

"Want me to get on to the hospital security bods and ask them to check the footage?" Bob asked.

"Why not? We've got nothing else to go on. Send them a photo of her while you're at it."

"Of course."

Sam sat at the nearest desk and placed her head in her hands. "Why is nothing ever simple around here? Jesus, if something has happened to her... I'm a fool. I should have put an officer outside the ward."

"Please don't go blaming yourself, boss. None of this is your fault."

Sam glanced at Claire and puffed out her cheeks. "Isn't it? Why do I feel like I've made a massive blunder, then?"

"Because you're human and you care. Plus, you're probably worried about your brother."

Sam shook her head and smiled. "I doubt whether it's the latter."

Bob joined them. "All done. They're going to get back to me ASAP."

"Great news. Where do we go from here?" Sam asked.

"I might have found something of relevance," Claire pitched in.

Sam rose from her seat and crossed the room. "What's that?"

"I told you that I had discovered nothing out of the ordinary about Jason's bank accounts; that was true, until now. Although, I'm unsure if it could be considered suspicious."

Sam smiled and gestured for Claire to get to the point.

"Sorry." She sighed and showed Sam her screen. "I've looked back and found that he transferred twenty grand into an ISA account two years ago. I don't know what made me do it, but I checked that account, and on the day of the fire, he withdrew all the money from it and closed it."

"Why would he do that? ISAs are supposed to be considered long-term financial accounts, aren't they?" Sam asked, not really having a clue as she was lucky if she had a couple of hundred floating around at any one time.

"Not necessarily," Claire corrected her. "My parents have stocks and shares ISAs that they add to every year. It's their safety-net money for their retirement. You're allowed to put away up to twenty grand tax-free each year. However, I believe you have access to that money at all times."

"Ah, I see. But why would he withdraw twenty grand from his account and disappear the same day?" Sam directed the question to her partner.

Bob shrugged. "Don't expect me to answer that."

Sam shook her head and perched on the desk next to Claire. "Come on, folks, we need to start thinking outside the box here. I believe it's the only way we're going to solve this case." She withdrew her phone and rang Oliver. "Have you seen Davina yet?"

"No sign of her, boss. We'll let you know if she comes back to the house. The handyman from the station has just arrived. The front door should be fixed soon."

"Okay, leave there when you can and return to base."

"Will do. Is everything all right, boss?"

"I wish. No, we're back to banging our heads against the wall here."

"Sorry to hear that. It's been a frustrating few days for us all."

"You're not wrong. See you soon." Sam pressed the END button, only for her mobile to ring again immediately. "DI Sam Cobbs. How…"

"Yadda, yadda. I know the spiel by now. It's Des."

"Oh, hi. Please tell me you have some good news for me? We're losing the will to live here."

"That bad, eh? I'm not sure if it can be classed as good, but I do have some news for you."

"I'm all ears."

"Warren Goldman isn't the father of the unborn child."

"What the…? Shit! That's put the cat amongst the pigeons. Are you sure?"

"I'm going to forget you said that. I have to fly. I promised I would get back to you as soon as I knew the results."

"I appreciate it, thanks, Des."

He abruptly hung up on her. She should have expected it. She poked her tongue out at her phone.

Amused by her antics, Bob asked, "What did he say to warrant you doing that?"

"He told me that the DNA test he ran on the baby has confirmed that Warren isn't the father."

"Okay," Bob said slowly as he thought. "So that must mean that Jason was the father."

Sam shook her head. "How can he be when Vanessa told us he's infertile? Or was she lying?"

"Bugger, I forgot that. What if he is?"

"Then we have to assume that someone else was the father and Helen had more than one lover on the go," Sam admitted.

"Holy shitballs. What tangled webs we weave!"

"You could say that. I can't sit around here doing nothing. Let's get on the road, Bob. I could do with some fresh air."

"Where are we going?"

"I'll have a word with Nick on the way out. Remind him there's an alert out on Jason's car. Should we do one for Davina's as well?"

"No, we gave her a lift to the hospital, so her car should still be outside her house."

"Excellent point. I'd forgotten all about that."

"While we're out, we could drop by Jason's parents' house, or had you forgotten about that, too?"

"Yes, it had slipped my mind. Christ, I've got so much going on up there, some things are bound to get pushed to the back and overlooked."

"If you say so."

"Okay, let's go. Keep digging, Claire, see what other nuggets of information you can come up with for us. We'll be back soon."

AFTER SAM RAN through her needs with the desk sergeant, they left the station. She didn't know which way to turn at the exit to the car park.

"What's wrong?"

"I'm listening to my gut, and it hasn't communicated to me which direction to take yet."

"For fuck's sake," Bob muttered.

"I heard that. Here it is. I've got my answer now. It's this way."

"Where are we going first?"

"It's a surprise. Wait and see."

Halfway through the journey, Bob announced, "Why are you going to Davina's house?"

"Call it curiosity."

He folded his arms and grunted his disapproval.

Oliver and Liam seemed surprised to see them when Sam drew up alongside them. "I take it the SOCO techs have left now?"

"About five minutes ago. No sign of Davina."

"I believe she'd show up in a taxi. As Bob reminded me earlier, we gave her a lift to the hospital."

"Ah, right. That makes sense then. Want us to check around the back? We haven't done that yet."

"No. You get back to the station. Bob and I will have a shufti."

He gave her a front door key. "In case you need it. We were going to hand it in to the desk sergeant. I've left one with the neighbour on the right as well, just in case Davina turned up."

"Good thinking. Thanks, lads. See you back at the station. We shouldn't be too long."

Oliver and Liam both gave her a thumbs-up and drove off. Sam parked in the spot they vacated, which was opposite Davina's house.

"Come on, fess up. What are we really doing here?"

Sam winked at him and exited the vehicle. She was halfway across the road when he decided to get out of the car and join her.

"You took your time." She pressed her key fob to lock the vehicle and inserted the key Oliver had given her into Davina's front door.

"What are you doing? She's not here, Sam."

"I know that. Bear with me. I haven't lost my mind, not yet. At least I hope not," she said and entered the hallway.

"God, you can be so frustrating at times, especially when you keep me in the dark like this."

"Two minutes, that's all." Sam pushed open the door to the front room, which was the lounge. It was decorated in a modern style, featuring an abundance of chrome and silver. Accents of teal added a pop of colour in the curtains and cushions. "This looks freshly kitted out, wouldn't you agree?"

"Unless there's a receipt attached to everything, I'm not sure how you can tell that."

Sam sniffed the air. "I used my nose. I can smell it's been newly painted."

"What do you want? A prize for being right?"

She chuckled and walked towards the photos on the mantelpiece. She lifted them one by one. They were mostly of Helen and Jason, although there was one of her parents tucked at the back. The photo that really caught her attention was the one someone else had taken of Helen, Jason and Davina, which confirmed her suspicions. "As I suspected."

"What is?"

She snapped a photo of it with her phone and then handed the silver frame to Bob. "What do you make of it?"

"Is this a trick question?"

"Study, really study it, and tell me what you see."

He ran a hand around his face and sighed. "I'm too tired for this shit, Sam. What am I looking at?"

"You're hopeless. The way she's looking at Jason."

"Who?"

"Davina. Good Lord, why do I always have to point out the obvious to you?"

"That's unfair. Bloody hell, you're right. Hey, wait a minute, he's her brother-in-law. She's bound to think affectionately about him, isn't she?"

Sam sped out of the room and up the stairs to the bedroom, where they had found Davina covered in blood. She pulled on a glove, rummaged through the bedside drawers and discovered the woman's diary, which was locked.

"What are you searching for, Sam? I wish you'd come right out with it and tell me what you suspect."

"Why would she lock her diary if she's the only person in the house?"

"I don't know, perhaps out of habit of sharing a room with her sister when they were growing up."

"Maybe. Alternatively, she's made sure Helen didn't read it if she came to visit her."

"Why?"

Sam rolled her eyes and reached for the pen she saw in the drawer. She wedged it under the lock and tried to prise it open, but she failed.

"Give it here. Let me have a go at it." Bob snatched it out of her hand and, with very little effort, successfully snapped the strap secured by the lock. "Oh, dear. I think I broke it."

"A case of not knowing how strong you are, eh?"

He grinned and handed Sam the diary. She flicked through it to the night of the fire. There were only two words written under that date: *Job done*. She showed it to Bob.

"What the fuck? What's she referring to? The fire?"

Sam nodded. Her gaze shifted to the Ali Baba-type laundry basket at the side of the wardrobe. The second she lifted the lid, the smell hit her. Replacing it, she said, "Have a whiff and tell me what you can smell."

"Do I really want to stick my nose in a woman's laundry basket?"

"Stop messing about and do it."

He bent over and she lifted the lid. "Jesus. Petrol."

"Exactly."

"She couldn't have done it, could she? Killed her own sister? Why?"

"Three guesses."

He shook his head as the realisation dawned. "Because she loved Jason. What about the twenty grand?"

"One thing at a time. Bugger, I bet all this was a frigging ruse. She's been taking us for fools throughout the investigation. Her parents warned us what she was like."

"So they did. We should have picked up on that earlier. What now?"

"Now the hunt begins for Davina." She withdrew an evidence bag she always carried in her pocket and slipped the diary inside. Sam ran towards the door.

Bob remained still, seemingly perplexed. "Do you think she's hurt Jason?"

Sam crossed the room again and rubbed his upper arm. "Honestly, I don't know, mate. It's up to us to find out."

"What about putting a trace on his phone?"

"It's got to be worth a try. Maybe we should have actioned that a while ago. Sorry, partner, I just thought Jason had gone to ground, you know, after losing everything."

"The thought didn't cross my mind either. Sam, I'm worried. What if she's kidnapped him, or worse still, killed him?"

"Try not to consider the worst. Come on, let's get back to the station."

Sam used her siren to ease them through the traffic that was building because of school kicking out time. "Bummer, we usually avoid being on the road during this time of day."

They arrived back at the station, and bolted up the stairs. Sam clapped to gain the rest of the team's attention while Bob made the call to get Jason's phone tracked.

"Here's what I think is going on, folks. Feel free to chip in if you disagree. It's not like we've got dozens of options open to us. Bob and I took a look around Davina's house. Something in my gut was telling me that we'd missed something when we rescued her. In the lounge, we found the usual family photos on display. However, one of them stood out like a sore thumb. Bob couldn't see it at first until I pointed it out to him, but I digress." She withdrew her phone and handed it to Claire. "What do you make of it?"

Claire gasped. "Shit. You're right."

Sam collected the phone and gave it to Oliver and Liam to look at.

"Holy crap!" Oliver said.

"I see it, too," Liam replied.

"I'm glad I'm not working with a bunch of idiots. Then we searched her bedroom. The bloodstained carpet told a different story to what else we found. In her bedside table—you'll need to pull on a glove for this, folks—I discovered her diary, which was locked. Bob worked his magic and broke into it for me. I flicked through to the day of the fire and found this." Again, she offered the diary to Claire first, who glanced up at Sam and shook her head.

Then Sam gave the diary to Oliver.

"What the...?"

"How could we have missed it?" Liam asked.

"Because she manipulated us. She's been doing it from day one. Her parents haven't got a good thing to say about her. That should have been a red flag for me, but it wasn't."

"Don't do it, boss," Claire said. "You can't blame yourself. The whole team missed it."

Sam covered her eyes with her hand as the tears pricked at them. She shook her head several times. "I should have realised sooner. Now Jason could be in danger."

"We'll get her. She won't get away from us again," Oliver said with more confidence than Sam was feeling right now.

"Let's hope so. Bob is running a trace on Jason's phone. She's probably holding him hostage somewhere right under our noses, knowing how much she enjoys toying with us. What a bitch! I can't wait to get my hands on her and wrap them around her throat. Wishful thinking on my part, but you know what I mean. She's the lowest of the low. To kill her sister because she was after her husband."

"Maybe she saw him as fair game," Claire chipped in. "After she found out about his affair with Vanessa."

Sam tapped the side of her nose and then pointed at Claire. "Maybe that's when she hatched her plan. I wish I knew what part the twenty grand had to play in all of this. I can sense it has something to do with the investigation, but what?"

"Maybe Jason got wind of what she was up to and tried to pay her off?" Liam suggested.

"Possibly. Anything we come up with will be pure speculation until we find either Jason or Davina. Come on, Bob. Hurry up. Time is of the essence now."

Sam's phone rang. She recognised the number and groaned. "DI Sam Cobbs. How may I help you?"

"Inspector, this is Matthew Baldwin. Do you have any news for us?"

"I'm sorry, it's too soon for that, Mr Baldwin."

"I don't wish to pester you. I realise you're doing your best, but Linda and I are here, twiddling our thumbs. We're eager to know what's happened to our daughter, as you can imagine."

"We're doing our best to find her, sir, I promise you. As soon as I finished speaking to you earlier, a member of my team spoke with a security officer who is checking the footage at the hospital. If Davina left with anyone, then we'll soon find out. I'll call you if any news comes our way. I've also issued an alert for her, so every patrol in the area will be keeping an eye open for your daughter. Trust us, my team and I won't let you down."

"We do. If we think of anywhere she might have gone, we'll call you."

"That would be a great help. Thank you." Sam swallowed as she ended the call. "Bugger, I had trouble biting my tongue."

Bob rejoined the conversation. "All actioned. They're checking Jason's and Davina's phones for us. Is everything all right?"

"Let's hope they come up trumps. I could do without Davina's parents ringing me every ten minutes to check if their daughter has been located. I nearly broke out in a sweat while I was talking to Mr Baldwin."

"In case you let it slip about your theory?"

Sam nodded and walked over to prepare the coffee. "I'm in dire need of a caffeine overload. Did the techs mention how long they're likely to be getting back to you?"

"It won't be for another hour or two. Surprise, surprise, they've got a backlog of tasks to get through."

"Did you tell them how urgent it is?"

"Of course I did." Bob sounded offended by her question.

He helped her hand around the drinks, then Sam went through

to her office to tackle her post. After flicking through the pile awaiting her, she set it aside and called Rhys.

"Sorry I didn't ring at lunchtime. We've been up to our eyes in crap today."

"No need to apologise. You sound stressed. Are you?"

"I've had to deal with a personal issue today, as well as frustrating elements of the investigation. I'll tell you about it later."

"Is your father okay?"

"Yes, he's fine. Honestly, it's nothing to worry about, and I have a stack of work vying for my attention. I also wanted to warn you that I might be late home this evening."

"Can I ask why?"

"We're waiting on a call from the tech team. They're tracing a few phones for us. Once that information comes through, we'll be setting off to track them down."

"Sounds ominous. Keep me informed, if you can."

"I will. Take care. I love you."

"Love you, too. Stay alert, Sam."

"Don't worry about me. I'll be fine."

Sam had knuckled down after that and was coming to the end of one of the longest hours of the day, but she still had a few emails she needed to respond to before she could walk away from her desk.

Bob poked his head around the door. "Are you free?"

"It depends on whether you have any news for me."

"I do."

"I'll come out. I've seen enough of these four walls for one day."

She tidied up the papers and swiftly followed her partner out of the room. "Please tell me the techs have traced the phones?"

"They have. They're together."

Sam tipped her head back and looked at the ceiling. She punched the air and said, "I knew I was right. What a bitch! She's led us a merry dance since the day we met her. Where are they?"

Bob pulled a face. "At Jason's parents' house."

She growled and punched her thigh. "Which we were supposed to check earlier but didn't get around to it. Okay, let's get over there. Oliver and Liam, you join us. We'll grab some Tasers on the way out and assess whether we need to call for an ART once we're at the location."

Bob removed his jacket from the back of his chair and said, "That bitch is going to pay for what she's done."

"I'll make sure of it," Sam agreed.

9

Sam was silent throughout the journey, her head swirling with different scenarios about how this might go down now. "She's obviously unstable, isn't she?"

"I guess she must be, to fool the doctors into thinking she'd lost her sight. What a devious bitch."

"I still have an inkling this isn't going to end well. When we get there, your job will be to keep a close eye on Jason. Leave Davina to me, got that?"

"If you insist. You mean if he's still alive?"

"Don't even go there, Bob. He's alive. I doubt if she will kill him, not unless we push her to her limits. I don't intend to do that. However, we all know what happens with best-laid plans."

"I do. Now I'm worried about Jason's safety."

Sam glanced at the satnav. They had another five minutes' drive before they reached their destination. "Have you been here before?"

"Yes, I came to a barbecue they held for an anniversary party a few years ago."

"Can you give me a brief layout of the place? By that I mean, is it detached? What are the surroundings like?"

"Yes, it's a detached house in a cul-de-sac with about six to eight other houses. From what I can remember, the house is at the back of the close, with two immediate neighbours, one on each side."

"That's perfect. What about the garden at the rear? Can you tell me if it's enclosed, has fields beyond perhaps?"

"Gosh, now you're testing me." He shook his head. "I can't tell you for definite, Sam, sorry."

"No need to be sorry. I wanted to get everything planned out before we get there, in case things escalate quickly upon our arrival."

"Don't say that. I'm nervous enough as it is."

Sam patted his thigh to reassure him. "Don't be. We've got this, matey. Keep the faith."

"I'm hoping—no, praying—that he's still alive."

"PMA, remember that at all times." She glanced in her rearview mirror to check that the boys were still with them.

"I THINK we should leave the cars at the end of the cul-de-sac and creep up to the house on foot," Bob said.

Sam agreed. It was a small collection of houses, not what she'd expected from his description. "They're closer than I anticipated."

"Sorry if I misled you."

"You didn't. Come on, let's make our move." Sam retrieved her Taser from the glove box and exited the vehicle.

Oliver had his Taser in his right hand down by his side.

"Are you ready? We'll sneak up on them. Once we're closer, Liam, I need you to creep up to the house, see what you can make out through the front windows. If they're not there, we'll go round the back of the property and check there. Please, please, don't let them see you. As soon as you've assessed the situation, come back immediately."

Liam raised his thumb. "Got it, boss. You can count on me."

"I know I can. In the meantime, we'll get closer, ready to pounce if necessary. Go."

Liam ran towards the house at the rear of the estate. He crouched low and moved like a territorial cat towards the ground-floor front window. He craned his neck to peer through the bottom corner of the window.

Sam, Bob and Oliver followed him but held back. They waited outside the neighbour's gate. She was hoping the neighbours weren't nosey and stayed inside their homes until the manoeuvre was over.

Liam rushed back to them. "Jason is alive. She's got him tied to a chair. I heard shouting. She's in his face. To me, she seems on the edge, as if she's about to do something silly."

"I'm getting in there, now," Bob said.

Sam tugged on his arm as he pushed past her. "You're not. You do that and Jason will be killed. She's obviously prepared to kill him now. We've got to prevent that from happening." She glanced at the house and saw the gate at the side. "I think we should see what's around the back. It might be easier to get in around there. Are we all in agreement?"

Oliver and Liam both nodded.

Bob was straining to make the move. "Yes, let's get in there. Before it's too late."

"You're going to need to calm down first, Bob," Sam warned. "Take a few deep breaths, and then we'll make our move."

Bob did as instructed and announced, "I'm ready. Please, don't delay this. Jason's in trouble in there, and it sounds like she's on the brink of losing it."

"We're going now. Follow my lead. That goes for all of you. I don't want any heroics in there. One false move on our part and… I don't have to finish that sentence, do I?" Sam led the way on tiptoes down the driveway, sticking to the strips of concrete on either side of the gravel. She hooked her hand over the top of the gate and wiggled the bolt silently. She closed her eyes, dreading the gate might squeak. It didn't. So they proceeded. There was decking outside the back door. She turned to the others and held a finger to her lips. "Quietly, you hear me?"

The three men nodded.

Sam tried the handle on the back door. Thankfully, it wasn't locked. She opened it carefully, once again, hoping, that the hinges were well oiled. The four of them entered the house. Sam cringed when Davina screamed at Jason, calling him vile names. Sam closed her eyes to control her racing heart and then crept closer to the door that would take them through to the hallway. She checked behind her; her team was eager to get in there to tackle Davina, but Sam sensed it would be wiser not to make any drastic moves.

She listened for a moment or two, and then, when she thought it was safe enough to continue, she entered the hallway. Davina's constant screams were driving her insane, and she was left wondering how Jason was coping under the barrage of abuse the deranged woman was dishing out.

A whack sounded in the room. Sam gestured for the team to go. They raced into the lounge to find Davina standing behind Jason with a ten-inch blade to his throat.

"Davina, the game is up. Don't do anything rash that you're likely to regret."

"What the fuck are you doing here? How did you get in?" Davina's gaze flitted between the four of them and then jumped back to Sam. "Get them out of here or he gets it."

Sam had tucked her Taser into the back of her trousers before they'd entered the house. She raised her hands. "Let's talk about this. Why don't you let Jason go now? He's done nothing wrong."

"Are you kidding me? He's the reason I did all of this."

"Because you love him?" Sam asked, her tone gentle and persuasive.

"Yes."

"We can work this out, Davina. Please, let me go," Jason said, his eyes imploring Sam and the team to help him.

"Shut up. You'll speak when you're spoken to." As if enforcing her threat, Davina nicked his throat with the blade.

Jason winced as a narrow dribble of blood trickled down his neck. "No, please don't. I won't say another word, I promise."

Sam could see how terrified Jason was. Her heart went out to him. But it was Bob's reaction she was eager to keep a watchful eye on, as well. He was prone to jumping into situations feetfirst. "Why don't you put the weapon down and we'll discuss this further, Davina?"

"I don't want to discuss anything. I want him to tell you that he loves me and he agreed to do away with his wife."

"Your sister, Helen. Is this true, Jason?"

He closed his eyes. "I suppose so."

Yet another twist in the tale. *Is that what's going on here? He persuaded Davina to kill Helen on the pretence that they would be together and then cast her aside.* Sam wasn't sure. It seemed too wicked for a reasonable human being to consider. *Did he underestimate the power of Davina's love for him and her capabilities, only for it to backfire?* "Is that what happened? He led you to believe you had a future together?"

Davina nodded. "He told me he would ditch Vanessa and we'd be together. But first I had to kill Helen."

Sam knew it was the truth because Jason refused to look at her. "And the twenty thousand?"

"He told me to use it as a deposit on a new house."

"And what went wrong?" Sam asked, intrigued.

"I wasn't supposed to burn the house down, only create a fire that would have been put out easily by the fire brigade."

"But you used an accelerant, which meant the fire got out of control quickly. You were the person standing on the corner before the fire, weren't you?"

She nodded. "Yes. He promised me the earth, but once Helen was dead, he turned against me. Told me that he was starting over with Vanessa. I showed him how much I loved him, and he threw it back in my face. He used me as a means to an end. He didn't have the balls to kill his wife, so he persuaded me to do it for him."

"Is this right, mate?" Bob demanded.

The fact that Jason couldn't look at Bob spoke volumes.

"Jesus. I thought I knew you. You disgust me." Bob grunted and left the room.

Sam was torn. She was desperate to see how her partner was after the dramatic revelation, but she found herself glued to the spot, determined to reach a quick resolution to the situation. Harshly, if necessary, she no longer cared if Jason was hurt in the process. He'd not only deceived them, he'd done the unthinkable and lied to his best mate.

"Put the weapon down, Davina. He's already proven that he's not worth going to prison for. He used you."

"I know. Now I have to kill him. He's tried to persuade me to set him free so that we can be together. He's tied me up in knots, leading me to believe he has feelings for me. He's a scumbag. I didn't know him at all. He made me kill Helen and her unborn baby. He told me the baby wasn't his, that it was Warren's."

Sam shook her head. "We ran a DNA test on the baby. It's not Warren's. Either Helen had another lover on the go, or the baby was Jason's."

The unexpected news grabbed Jason's attention. "What? It can't be. I've been told I'm infertile."

"We'll run another DNA test and see what that comes up with. Doctors have been wrong in the past. If that's the case, you've not only carried out a plan to kill your wife, but you've also succeeded in killing your unborn child."

Tears welled up in his eyes. "Get this woman away from me. I need to grieve. I can't do that with a knife at my throat."

"Don't listen to him," Davina said. "He doesn't give a shit about anyone else. He's selfish to the core."

Sam sensed Davina was going to do something foolish. She withdrew her Taser and aimed it at her. Oliver followed her lead and did the same.

"Put the knife down or we'll fire. Let the courts deal with him, Davina. They'll listen to you if you tell them how he manipulated and coerced you into killing Helen."

"Will they? He's got a way with words. He can twist people around his little finger. We'd be better off without him."

Davina glanced down at the knife, and Sam took the shot. The woman collapsed to the floor. Liam rushed forward to check her status. Sam released her finger, and Liam removed the wires from Davina's chest.

Not caring if Jason was hurt or not, Sam left Oliver to deal with him while she went in search of her partner. Bob had his hands resting on the kitchen table. She stood beside him and placed an arm around his shoulders.

"Are you all right? We should call for backup to take them in."

"A car is on the way, and no, I'm not all right. If you must know, I feel a damn fool. I trusted him, and in the process, I let you down."

"Don't be silly. You could never do that."

Oliver and Liam left the house with the suspects via the front door.

"Bob, talk to me," Jason shouted.

Bob tensed up beside her. "He's lucky I don't kill him myself. How could he do it, Sam? Kill his wife like that?"

"He didn't. He persuaded Davina to do it. Furthermore, he killed his child as well."

"We don't know if it's his, though, not yet."

"Trust me, it's his. My female intuition is telling me it is. He's ended up tangling a web that even he couldn't see the outcome of." She turned her partner to face her and hugged him. "I'm sorry he let you down, Bob."

"He was my best mate. Words fail me at this moment. Don't leave me alone in a room with him. I don't think I'll be able to control myself."

"And who could blame you? This is the ultimate betrayal, hon. Come on, let's get them processed. They can both sweat it out in a cell tonight. We'll go to the pub and drink to our success as usual. I know and appreciate how hard this has been for you, Bob. You're going to have to let it go, otherwise it's going to eat away at you."

He sighed and secured the back door with the key. "I know. It ain't gonna be easy. Bloody hell, we've been inseparable over the years. I've always treated him like a brother. I feel sick to my stomach."

"I'm sure. Don't let him get to you. He'll get what's coming to him. I promise you."

The patrol car had arrived. Oliver was assisting one of the officers to put Jason in the back. Davina was already in the rear seat of his car.

"I'm glad neither of them is travelling back with us. I couldn't have handled that," Bob said.

Sam rubbed his arm. "You made the right call, asking for backup to join us."

They secured the front door on their way out and drove back to the station. Sam kept quiet during the journey, sensing Bob had a few issues he needed to sort out internally.

When they arrived, Davina was causing havoc in the reception area until Sam jumped in and asked Nick to process Jason first while they stayed with Davina.

"Take a seat," Sam ordered.

Davina stared at her defiantly and narrowed her eyes. "Don't boss me around."

Bob took a step forward.

Sam clasped his arm. "Ignore her."

Davina threw herself into one of the chairs and crossed her arms.

An officer stood beside Davina in case she decided to escape.

Sam and Bob waited opposite her until they got the all-clear from Nick to take Davina down to the custody sergeant to be charged.

They delivered the mouthy Davina and returned to the incident room. It was gone five, and Sam was weary as sin.

"I'm calling it. Pack up, folks. I think we deserve a drink after the week we've had. Make the necessary calls to your families and join me over the road."

The team all jumped into action, except for Bob.

"Hey, I thought going to the boozer would have put a smile on your face."

He rolled his eyes. "I can't get over the betrayal. I might give the pub a miss. This has knocked the shit out of me, Sam."

Sam sighed. "I'm not blind. Don't let him win. People change. Maybe that's the case with Jason, and you've been too busy over the years to notice it. I'm gutted that he betrayed you."

"Abigail will be rejoicing."

"I doubt if that's true. Why?"

"Because she's always told me she thought there was something dodgy about him."

"Ouch! And you refused to listen."

"We've been mates since our teens. What was I supposed to do? Dump him just because my wife didn't like him?"

Sam shrugged. "Come on. Maybe things will look better after you throw a pint down your neck."

The team switched off their computers and, together, they left the station and crossed the road to the Red Lion. Sam bought the first round and made the toast.

"To a job well done. We overcame the obstacles put in our way and still came out on top."

Everyone, including Bob, chinked their glasses together. Sam watched her partner carefully over the next ten minutes. He was withdrawn, twisting his pint glass on the table rather than joining in the conversation.

She nudged him with her knee. "Come on, Bob, this isn't like you. I feel useless right now. I hate to see you suffering like this."

"I need time, Sam. I'm going home. Enjoy yourselves, my heart isn't in it." With that, he marched out of the pub.

Sam finished off her drink and left not long after to see his vehicle pulling out of the station's car park. She drove home, unsure how to proceed with making things right for him.

"As if I haven't got enough on my plate already."

When she arrived home, she found Rhys preparing their meal in the kitchen.

"Hey. How was your day?"

"Good and bad. Do you fancy a walk?"

Both dogs rushed out of their baskets, their tails wagging furiously.

"We've not long got back. Are you okay?"

"They're both up for it. I could do with some fresh air. Will dinner spoil if we leave it?"

"You win. I can leave it simmering."

They set off, the dogs eagerly pulling on their leads as if they hadn't been walked in days.

They reached the park before Rhys plucked up the courage to speak to her. "Does this have to do with the personal issue you've had to deal with today?"

"Yes. Sorry I blanked you earlier. It's been a full-on day, and I hadn't had time to process it fully, therefore, I couldn't tell you exactly how I felt about the situation."

"Now you have me intrigued. What situation, Sam? Is everyone all right?"

"Yes, sort of. Here I go again. Right, I'll tell you what happened from the beginning." She watched the dogs chasing each other around the park as she retold the events of the day that had concerned her family.

"Oh heck. I'm not surprised you've been in turmoil. How is he?"

"I need to check in with Crystal. I'll do that after dinner. I apologise for keeping you out of the loop, I didn't mean to. It's just that on top of everything else that has gone on today with the investigation…"

"Stop tying yourself into knots. I'm fine about it. How did he react to seeing you?"

"No different to the last time I saw him. He was angry, sarcastic, pretty brutal really. That's why I left. I made an excuse that I had to get back to work, I think. The day has flown past in a blur."

He hugged her. "I'm always here for you, Sam."

"I know you are, and I appreciate that more than you'll ever know."

"Maybe we should visit him at the hospital tomorrow before he goes back to prison. You know, for your own peace of mind. I believe you'll find the exercise healing, especially if I'm there to hold your hand."

"I'll have to think about that. Are you sure you want to meet him?"

"I'm intrigued, purely from a professional point of view."

Sam laughed. "On your head be it, then. He's the total opposite to the rest of us."

He grinned. "Then I'll definitely look forward to meeting him.

What's happened with your investigation?" He whistled the dogs to heel, slipped on their leads, and they began the walk back home.

Sam ran through the bullet points of what had emerged throughout the day. Rhys was shocked.

"Wowser! How could that conniving woman do that to her own sister? And he's no better, leading her astray like that. Have you had a chance to interview either of them yet?"

"No, I have that pleasure to come in the morning. It's Bob I feel sorry for; this has hit him badly."

"I'm not surprised. The betrayal of a dear friend can be devastating. Tell him if he needs to chat, I'm available and I won't even charge him."

She kissed his cheek. "Thank you. I'll pass the message on. Hopefully he'll be in a better frame of mind tomorrow. Enough about work—or should I say my work? How was your day?"

"Peaceful and uneventful in comparison."

They both laughed and wended their way back to the house to enjoy the bolognaise he'd prepared for them.

EPILOGUE

Sam decided to exclude Bob from the interviews because, in her opinion, his frame of mind hadn't improved overnight. Although he was upset about the decision, he accepted that Sam knew best.

Instead, Sam asked Oliver to join her for the interviews. Once the duty solicitor arrived, they began with Jason. Sam was determined to keep her feelings suppressed during the interview.

Oliver said the necessary verbiage for the recording, then Sam asked her first question.

"Why, Jason? Why did you arrange for your wife to be killed?"

As expected, he showed little to no emotion throughout the interview and said nothing else other than what his solicitor had advised him to say: "No comment."

After another ten minutes, Sam asked the officer also present in the room to escort Jason back to his cell. She followed them down the corridor to the reception area. "Hi, Nick. Any chance we can swap the officers over?"

"I'll get a female to join you, ma'am. How did it go?"

"It didn't. Not really. Hopefully, we'll get more out of Davina."

"I'll fetch her myself. Do you want me to bring some drinks in?"

"Maybe some water. I'm not sure I could trust her with a hot drink in her hand while I wind her up."

He cringed and nodded. "You're right. I hadn't thought about that. I'll be two minutes."

Sam used the time to call the hospital to check on her brother's status. The nurse told her he seemed brighter today and that her sister was there, visiting him. She thanked the nurse and hung up. She was upset that her sister hadn't told her about closing her business to be with Mike at the hospital. She shrugged it off and returned to the interview room.

Mr Aldridge, the duty solicitor, fidgeted in his seat. "I should have ten minutes with Miss Baldwin before the interview begins."

"Of course, as long as you don't tell her to go down the usual frustrating route of 'no comment', because it doesn't really help when we're trying to get to the bottom of why someone would set out to kill their own sister."

He smirked and replied, "I can't promise that."

Sam and Oliver left the room and dipped next door, not wanting to watch Davina walk down the corridor towards them.

"It's not going well, is it, boss?"

"So far, it's turned out the way I expected it to. Hopefully, if I wind Davina up enough, as is my intention, she'll ignore the advice Aldridge is giving her in there and reveal the truth. If not, it'll be up to us to come up with a convincing case against her."

"I'm sure we'll be able to do that, given time."

Sam glanced at her watch. "They've had more than enough time to get acquainted. Let's go."

Davina glared at Sam as Oliver started the recording. "Would you care to enlighten us as to what state of mind you were in when you rang the doorbell at your sister's house on the night you set fire to it?"

"I was of sound mind," Davina responded, earning herself an angry tut from Aldridge.

"And when you bashed your sister several times with a heavy object?"

"Yes, the same."

It was enough, in Sam's opinion, to put the final nail in her coffin. It meant that further down the line, Davina couldn't pull the insanity card out of the bag like most suspects did these days.

"Would you care to share with us the reason why you killed your sister?"

Aldridge coughed and leaned in to whisper in Davina's ear.

She stared at Sam and said, "No comment."

"What happened between you and Jason for you to want to turn on him and hold a knife against the throat of the man you loved?"

Davina glared at Sam, and then a smirk pulled her lips apart. "No comment."

"You were never held hostage at your house, were you?"

"No comment."

"The concussion and blindness you suffered were a sham, too, weren't they? You fooled not only us but the doctors at the hospital, too. How devious, how low can someone go?"

Davina grinned. "No comment."

Sam fired question after question at her, in the hope that she could break the woman down, but Davina held firm.

Eventually, Sam put an end to the futile game Davina was determined to control, and she announced that the interview was over.

The officer escorted Davina to her cell, and Sam showed the duty solicitor back to the reception area. She gave him a curt goodbye and then returned to the incident room to fill in the rest of the team.

"What we've got to do is ensure neither of them gets away with this, peeps. We need to work like Trojans to find every piece of evidence we can to nail both of them. I'm going to get on to the lab and make sure they cross all the T's at their end, too. Bob, will you join me in my office?"

"If I have to," he complained and followed her. He closed the door behind them.

Once they were both seated, Sam asked, "How are you?"

"About the same. I know I've got to get over it. It's just difficult for me right now."

"What if you took a few days off? Would that help?"

"Not really, because then I'd have Abigail bending my ears out of shape."

She smiled. "Rhys said if you need to chat, off the record, you should give him a call. I think it might be a good idea, mate."

At first, he seemed shocked by the idea, but then his expression changed. "Maybe I should take him up on his offer. Would he have time today?"

Sam winked. "I think you're doing the right thing. I'll call him, see when he can fit you in."

He left the room.

Sam rang Rhys. "Bob has told me he'd love to have a chat with you if you can squeeze him in."

"That's great news. I'm happy to oblige. What about eleven this morning? Umm... I've also cleared my diary this afternoon. I thought we might go to the hospital to visit your brother. What do you think?"

Sam felt trapped all of a sudden. "If that's what you want to do. What about two o'clock? Is that okay with you?"

"Excellent. Do you want to pick me up? It's on the way."

"Sounds good to me. I'll send Bob to see you this morning. See you later. Love you."

SAM PICKED up Rhys at two on the dot. She kissed him and asked, "How did it go with Bob?"

Rhys raised his eyebrows. "Now, Sam, you know I can't tell you that."

"I didn't mean for you to go into details. I meant, did he open up to you? Enough to start the healing process?"

"You'll be pleased to know he did. Now that's the end of that conversation."

"Yes, boss." She let out the deepest sigh. "I can't say I'm looking forward to our visit."

"You'll be fine, because I'll be right there beside you."

She smiled, the dread seeping through her veins. *I can do this. All I have to do is keep a smile on my face, no matter what Mike flings at me.*

. . .

Sam parked the car, and they walked through the corridors, in silence, holding hands.

She showed her ID to the prison guard outside Mike's private room, glad to see the prison were doing their part in keeping the rest of the patients safe.

"You've got this," Rhys whispered in her ear when she paused before opening the door.

"Thanks. Here goes."

They entered the room. Crystal was sitting to the right of her brother. He was pale, but his eyes sparkled with something Sam struggled to distinguish when he laid eyes on her and Rhys.

"Hello, Mike. How are you feeling?"

"Rough. Aren't you going to introduce me to your next victim?"

"Mike, behave," Crystal warned.

Sam's blood boiled, and a knot tightened in her stomach. She glared at her brother, ignorant as usual.

Rhys approached the bed, his hand outstretched. "I'm Rhys, Sam's fiancé."

"Like I said, her next victim. You're aware she killed her last husband, aren't you?"

"Actually, she didn't. I was there when the incident happened," Rhys replied, his tone confident, ready to go into battle for the woman he loved.

"Whatever. Give her time. She's bound to let you down."

"Mike, that's not fair," Crystal said.

Her brother faced their sister and snapped, "Isn't it? Where was she when I needed her the most? She hid behind her badge and wanted nothing to do with me. Probably ashamed of what I had become."

Rhys raised his hand in front of him. "Look, Mike. I think you need to let go of the anger you're feeling. Sam has been worried sick since you were admitted. Give her a break."

"I find that hard to believe. She's too selfish to think about anyone but herself, always has been."

"Rhys, don't bother. He's not worth it. I've tried. My conscience is clear. I'm out of here." Sam opened the door and walked out.

"That's it. Do what you do best: turn your back on me, like you always do."

"You're sick," Rhys said. "She was prepared to put the past behind her, and you rejected her."

Rhys left the room. Sam was talking to the guard outside.

"Are you all right?" Rhys asked her.

"Yep, I'm done here. I should never have come."

"I agree. Some people in this life are beyond help."

They held hands and returned to the car.

Before they got in, she hugged him. "Thank you for sticking up for me back there."

"Why wouldn't I? You didn't do anything wrong, Sam. Let's forget about him and get on with our lives. I think it's time we put the finishing touches to our wedding plans, don't you?"

She touched his cheek. "If you still want me…"

"I do."

They sealed their conversation with a kiss.

THE END

THANK you for reading To Deceive Them, the next thrilling adventure is To Hurt Them.

While you're waiting for that to come out, have you read any of my other fast-paced crime thrillers yet?

WHY NOT TRY the first book in the DI Sara Ramsey series
No Right To Kill

. . .

OR GRAB the first book in the bestselling, award-winning, Justice series here, Cruel Justice

OR THE FIRST book in the spin-off Justice Again series,
   Gone in Seconds

PERHAPS YOU'D PREFER to try one of my other police procedural series, the DI Kayli Bright series which begins with
   The Missing Children

OR MAYBE YOU'D enjoy the DI Sally Parker series set in Norfolk,
   Wrong Place

OR MY GRITTY police procedural starring DI Nelson set in Manchester, Torn Apart

OR MAYBE YOU'D like to try one of my successful psychological thrillers I know The Truth or She's Gone or Shattered Lives

ALSO BY M A COMLEY

Blind Justice (Novella)

Cruel Justice (Book #1)

Mortal Justice (Novella)

Impeding Justice (Book #2)

Final Justice (Book #3)

Foul Justice (Book #4)

Guaranteed Justice (Book #5)

Ultimate Justice (Book #6)

Virtual Justice (Book #7)

Hostile Justice (Book #8)

Tortured Justice (Book #9)

Rough Justice (Book #10)

Dubious Justice (Book #11)

Calculated Justice (Book #12)

Twisted Justice (Book #13)

Justice at Christmas (Short Story)

Prime Justice (Book #14)

Heroic Justice (Book #15)

Shameful Justice (Book #16)

Immoral Justice (Book #17)

Toxic Justice (Book #18)

Overdue Justice (Book #19)

Unfair Justice (a 10,000 word short story)

Irrational Justice (a 10,000 word short story)

Seeking Justice (a 15,000 word novella)

Caring For Justice (a 24,000 word novella)

Savage Justice (a 17,000 word novella)

Justice at Christmas #2 (a 15,000 word novella)

Gone in Seconds (Justice Again series #1)

Ultimate Dilemma (Justice Again series #2)

Shot of Silence (Justice Again series #3)

Taste of Fury (Justice Again series #4)

Crying Shame (Justice Again series #5)

See No Evil (Justice Again series #6)

To Die For (DI Sam Cobbs #1)

To Silence Them (DI Sam Cobbs #2)

To Make Them Pay (DI Sam Cobbs #3)

To Prove Fatal (DI Sam Cobbs #4)

To Condemn Them (DI Sam Cobbs #5)

To Punish Them (DI Sam Cobbs #6)

To Entice Them (DI Sam Cobbs #7)

To Control Them (DI Sam Cobbs #8)

To Endanger Lives (DI Sam Cobbs #9)

To Hold Responsible (DI Sam Cobbs #10)

To Catch a Killer (DI Sam Cobbs #11)

To Believe the Truth (DI Sam Cobbs #12)

To Blame Them (DI Sam Cobbs 13)

To Judge Them (DI Sam Cobbs #14)

To Fear Him (DI Sam Cobbs #15)

To Deceive Them (DI Sam Cobbs #16)

To Hurt Them (DI Sam Cobbs #17)

Forever Watching You (DI Miranda Carr thriller)

Wrong Place (DI Sally Parker thriller #1)

No Hiding Place (DI Sally Parker thriller #2)

Cold Case (DI Sally Parker thriller #3)
Deadly Encounter (DI Sally Parker thriller #4)
Lost Innocence (DI Sally Parker thriller #5)
Goodbye My Precious Child (DI Sally Parker #6)
The Missing Wife (DI Sally Parker #7)
Truth or Dare (DI Sally Parker #8)
Where Did She Go? (DI Sally Parker #9)
Sinner (DI Sally Parker #10)
The Good Die Young (DI Sally Parker #11)
Coping Without You (DI Sally Parker #12)
Could It Be Him (DI Sally Parker #13)
Frozen In Time (DI Sally Parker #14)
Echoes of Silence (DI Sally Parker #15)
The Final Betrayal (DI Sally Parker #16)
Web of Deceit (DI Sally Parker Novella)
The Missing Children (DI Kayli Bright #1)
Killer On The Run (DI Kayli Bright #2)
Hidden Agenda (DI Kayli Bright #3)
Murderous Betrayal (Kayli Bright #4)
Dying Breath (Kayli Bright #5)
Taken (DI Kayli Bright #6)
The Hostage Takers (DI Kayli Bright Novella)
No Right to Kill (DI Sara Ramsey #1)
Killer Blow (DI Sara Ramsey #2)
The Dead Can't Speak (DI Sara Ramsey #3)
Deluded (DI Sara Ramsey #4)
The Murder Pact (DI Sara Ramsey #5)
Twisted Revenge (DI Sara Ramsey #6)
The Lies She Told (DI Sara Ramsey #7)

For The Love Of... (DI Sara Ramsey #8)

Run for Your Life (DI Sara Ramsey #9)

Cold Mercy (DI Sara Ramsey #10)

Sign of Evil (DI Sara Ramsey #11)

Indefensible (DI Sara Ramsey #12)

Locked Away (DI Sara Ramsey #13)

I Can See You (DI Sara Ramsey #14)

The Kill List (DI Sara Ramsey #15)

Crossing The Line (DI Sara Ramsey #16)

Time to Kill (DI Sara Ramsey #17)

Deadly Passion (DI Sara Ramsey #18)

Son of the Dead (DI Sara Ramsey #19)

Evil Intent (DI Sara Ramsey #20)

The Games People Play (DI Sara Ramsey #21)

Revenge Streak (DI Sara Ramsey #22)

Seeking Retribution (DI Sara Ramsey #23)

Gone... But Where? (DI Sara Ramsey #24)

Last Man Standing (DI Sara Ramsey #25)

Vanished (DI Sara Ramsey #26)

Shadows of Deception (DI Sara Ramsey #27)

I Know The Truth (A Psychological thriller)

She's Gone (A psychological thriller)

Shattered Lives (A psychological thriller)

Evil In Disguise – a novel based on True events

Deadly Act (Hero series novella)

Torn Apart (Hero series #1)

End Result (Hero series #2)

In Plain Sight (Hero Series #3)

Double Jeopardy (Hero Series #4)

Criminal Actions (Hero Series #5)

Regrets Mean Nothing (Hero series #6)

Prowlers (Di Hero Series #7)

Sole Intention (Intention series #1)

Grave Intention (Intention series #2)

Devious Intention (Intention #3)

Cozy mysteries

Murder at the Wedding

Murder at the Hotel

Murder by the Sea

Death on the Coast

Death By Association

Merry Widow (A Lorne Simpkins short story)

It's A Dog's Life (A Lorne Simpkins short story)

A Time To Heal (A Sweet Romance)

A Time For Change (A Sweet Romance)

High Spirits

The Temptation series (Romantic Suspense/New Adult Novellas)

Past Temptation

Lost Temptation

Clever Deception (co-written by Linda S Prather)

Tragic Deception (co-written by Linda S Prather)

Sinful Deception (co-written by Linda S Prather)

KEEP IN TOUCH WITH M A COMLEY

Newsletter
http://smarturl.it/8jtcvv

BookBub
www.bookbub.com/authors/m-a-comley

Blog
http://melcomley.blogspot.com

Facebook Readers' Page
https://www.facebook.com/groups/2498593423507951

TikTok
https://www.tiktok.com/@melcomley

Printed in Great Britain
by Amazon